JUDY HALLIWELL WASN'T DEAD YET.

She was very cold, on her back, her hands lying useless at her side, her mouth opening and closing like a fish out of water with the rain beating down on her. Then, she felt hands on her breasts stroking in a circular motion, a slight pressure at her waist; then she heard her zipper being pulled down. She felt hands tugging at her waistband, wrestling down the wet denim around her hips, taking her underwear with it.

She couldn't talk, but she could still think. She couldn't believe it—

SHE WAS GOING TO BE RAPED WHILE SHE DIED!

Books by Dane Hartman

Dirty Harry #1: Duel For Cannons
Dirty Harry #2: Death on the Docks
Dirty Harry #3: The Long Death
Dirty Harry #4: The Mexico Kill
Dirty Harry #5: Family Skeletons

Published by
WARNER BOOKS

DIRTY HARRY #5

Family Skeletons

Dane Hartman

WARNER BOOKS

A Warner Communications Company

WARNER BOOKS EDITION

Copyright © 1982 by Warner Books, Inc.
All rights reserved.

Warner Books, Inc., 75 Rockefeller Plaza, New York, N.Y. 10019

W A Warner Communications Company

Printed in the United States of America

First Printing: April, 1982

10 9 8 7 6 5 4 3 2 1

Dedication

For John Fullmer, who likes nothing better than slipping a .357 among the .38 rounds. May your Magnum never buck.

DIRTY HARRY #5

Family
Skeletons

Chapter One

Judy's parents had always thought it would be Arlene who got into trouble. If it had to be either of their daughters, Mr. and Mrs. Halliwell of Carlisle, Massachusetts, were afraid it would be the older one that they would get a police call about late one night.

Judy had always been the good girl. As often happens with the second-born of two children, Judy had always been the angelic one. Even when Arlene had sat on her and hit her about the head because she didn't want to share her toys, Judy had always borne out the blows in stoic consideration.

Even then, the younger child honestly seemed to understand what was fueling her sister's jealousy and sibling rivalry. As Judy got older, it got worse—or better, depending on one's point of view. All the area boys thought Arlene was getting better. The Halliwell parents thought Judy was getting better.

Somehow the younger daughter found equal time for athletic and scholastic pursuits. Her marks were always near the top of the class, and her folks never had to ask where at least one of their children were. While Arlene was out chasing and getting chased, Judy was always upstairs poring over her books. Her rewards were high school honors and a pair of round wire-rim glasses.

The spectacles did nothing to diminish Judy's petite

attractiveness, however. At sixteen she had developed as well as her sister in every dimension except height. But the boys did not clamor at her feet. Judy was not interested, and therefore was unapproachable. She made it clear that she found the whole high school mating ritual ridiculous. Arlene more than made up for Judy in that department.

While the elder girl pursued her peer-pressure obligations, Judy pursued other interests. While Arlene became a baton twirler and a cheerleader, Judy learned the flute and spent all her spare time doing volunteer charity work. She participated with the Pilgrim Fellowship at the family's church, and that is where she discovered her first true love. Only instead of a boy, it was the concepts of Unitarianism.

Judy loved the idea of a religion that used the whole realm of science, literature, art, and life as the field for its thought and inspiration. Arlene loved almost anything in a tight pair of Levis.

Judy worked selflessly in the name of the church: sending out brochures to interested citizens, contributing at the social events, candy-striping at the retirement home, and appearing to worship, come rain or shine, every Sunday. Arlene couldn't be bothered. She played pinball, went to movies, ate a lot of pizza, and made out.

When high school graduation led to college, Judy had plenty of options. Her final grades had been outstanding, and her parents were wealthy enough to send her any place she wanted to go. Rather than heading for the Midwest or California, Judy chose a university near her two major loves, her home and her church. She chose Emerson College in Boston, a liberal arts facility that concentrated on communication studies. Better than that, it was located on Beacon Street, right across from the Boston Common, and best of all, right down the street from the National Headquarters of the Unitarian Church.

Arlene didn't have much of a choice. She wanted to go

to NYU or UCLA, but neither would accept her. She wound up having to go to the one East Coast school that would admit her: the University of Bridgeport in the armpit of Connecticut.

For her freshman and sophomore years Judy maintained her high scholastic average in a speech major while spending every free minute inside the church offices on the outskirts of Beacon Hill. The years only enhanced the girl's growing beauty. She was extremely attractive in a perky way. She was still a bit short in comparison to other girls her age, but she was also nicely smooth and tightly shaped.

But no matter how good she looked, her social attitude did not change. Even the most patient of Unitarian reverends was disturbed by her increasingly intense devotion. But try as everyone might to arrange and send her out on dates, her main idea of a good time was her studies, her school, and her good Samaritanism.

Arlene more than made up for Judy socially, so their parents considered themselves blessed to have one daughter who was so popular and another who was so successful. As a reward for all her work, they moved Judy from the crowded, cramped Emerson dorm to a fourth-floor apartment of her very own on Beacon Hill's Mount Vernon Street—right around the corner from the Unitarian HQ. It was a pleasant one-bedroom apartment, made more pleasant by the many plants Judy hung around the bay window that looked out onto the narrow, lamp-lit, cobblestone street.

Whenever Judy wasn't at classes or the church, she was there, reading or cooking among her fauna, throw rugs, art prints, macramé, and cats. The big, bad city known as Beantown hadn't changed Judy in the slightest. She was still the same kind, unassuming, and infuriatingly sweet girl she had been all her life.

"For God's sake," Arlene had said to her during the summer vacation, "ease up. Give everybody a break. Live a little! What are you afraid of? That God'll get you for

11

having a little fun?" Then the older girl sang snatches of "Good Girls Don't," and "Only the Good Die Young," on her way out the door to visit a friend in the Big Apple.

Mr. and Mrs. Halliwell were worried. Arlene was living a little too fast. They had seen some horror movies on their pay-TV system and had seen the ads in the papers for all the others. And in each one, a wise-cracking, free-living, good-looking young woman just like their Arlene was stalked by a knife-wielding maniac. It scared them.

Subconsciously using the same guidelines for Judy didn't bother them as much. Judy was a good girl. She didn't smoke or drink or have sex. She was the solid, upstanding girl the movie murderers all missed. She was the one saved at the last minute.

In real life, things were different. They weren't so well scripted, and they could get a lot uglier. Mr. and Mrs. Halliwell learned that the hard way on a rainy Boston night at the beginning of Judy's third year at Emerson. It started with the scratching.

Judy, alone as usual except for her tank of tropical fish and her various pets, was reading a Doris Miles Disney novel while waiting for her homemade bread to rise in the oven. The rain hitting the bay windows was the only sound from outside until she became aware of a scratching noise rising above the sound of the bubbling of her aquarium.

It had to be a cat, she thought. It must've been one of her poor felines who accidentally got trapped on her apartment house rooftop. Judy closed the book and hurriedly counted the furry animals walking and resting around her living room. Ellery was missing. She had named him not for Ellery Queen, the great American detective hero, but for William Ellery Channing, the great Unitarian preacher and liberal reformer.

"Ellery," Judy called. She got up and walked into her bedroom. The cat wasn't there. "Ellery," she called, poking her head into the bathroom. The last place she looked was at the food bowls in the kitchen. Sure enough, Ellery was missing.

Judy shook her head in amusement. She found it cute, the mischief her pets managed to get in. Resigning herself to the fact that she had to go out on this chilly, wet night to rescue her cat, Judy went into the bedroom to change.

She took off her floral-printed kimono, finding a pair of jeans and a blue velour, V-necked pullover to go with it. She slipped them over her rounded frame and pulled on her cork-bottomed shoes. She went back and stood in the living room for a moment to get her bearings. She heard the scratching sound from above continue.

Insistent and persistent little devil, she thought. It must be the rain. The moisture must be driving the cat crazy. Shrugging, she pushed her keys into the pocket of her tight denims and went to the door.

"Don't go anywhere," she told her other pets. "I'll be right back."

She walked out into the hallway, closing the door behind her. She considered locking it. Naw, she thought, I'll only be gone a couple of seconds. Just to be on the safe side though, she looked downstairs over the banister. She could see no one. Just the comforting yellow lights of the hall and the deep rich brown **of** the wooden stairs and expensively papered walls. All she could hear was the scratching, growing no feebler. If anything, it was a little louder in the hall.

She followed the sound to the metal stairway that led to the door to the roof. The scratching was even clearer there.

"All right, Ellery, all right," she soothed, moving slowly up the steps. "Don't worry, I'm coming."

Judy placed one hand on the metal door latch and the other palm flat against the door. She twisted the latch and pushed the door open onto the blue-gray rain-streaked night.

Ellery had not done the scratching. The cat was incapa-

13

ble of doing anything in its condition except dying. It was lying in a drain by the edge of the roof, its stomach cut open, blood pumping down the rain pipe.

How Judy reacted marked all the differences between she and her sister. Arlene had seen all those crummy horror movies. She had sat in the theaters with her boyfriends' arms around her shoulders, jumping at all the right moments. But in the back of her mind, the older girl had been thinking how dumb all those screen heroines were. She wouldn't be so stupid as to run back into the house or hide in a closet or answer the door.

Her sister Judy didn't see movies much. She hadn't mentally prepared herself for possible horror. All she saw was one of her cats horribly wounded on the wet rooftop. It didn't dawn on her that he was too far from the door to have scratched it until she was already halfway to it.

The door closed behind her. She didn't hear the killer approach. Just as she neared Ellery's torn form, she felt the hand on her breast.

She looked down. A dark glove was squeezing on one side of her chest. Hard. She straightened in shock, throwing back her head to scream. The hand jerked up to clamp over her mouth. Her yell mingled into the howling wind as a low moan. She felt herself being pulled back— away from Ellery's body and the roof's edge. She raised her arms to slap away the hand crushing the lower part of her face. She couldn't reach it. Another arm was in the way.

She felt hot, panting breath on the back of her neck. She looked up at the sky, the stars blurred from the rain that splattered across her glasses. She sensed the other arm being pulled out of the way as she suddenly felt a tearing pain at her throat.

Then she was free. The attacker had released her. She stumbled forward, her hands moving up instinctively. She felt the moisture at her neck. She opened her mouth to cry as loudly as she could. All she heard was her own strangled gurgling. She brought her hands away from her throat, and they came away covered in red. Her eyes bulged. She saw the rain wash the blood from her hands as she felt her legs giving out from under her.

John Monahan was walking home from a movie at the Charles Street Theater complex. It was another lousy horror flick, *Just Before Dawn*. Another heart-warming saga of some young people being stalked and murdered by a raving lunatic with a big blade. Monahan, an Emerson sophmore majoring in film, shook his head in amazement. It was the post-summer slump, he realized. All the major studios had already released all their big summer hopefuls. The ones that stunk faded away. The ones that hit stayed to great box-office returns. As usual, there were more stinkers than hits.

So come fall, the theater owners were desperate to schedule any movie that was a sure money-maker. And these cheap little bloody numbers always made back their investment—usually because they were made for a dollar and a quarter in someone's backyard. Monahan marveled at it all. Why did he keep going back to movie after movie? They all had the same plots, the same shocks, and the same gore. What a waste of time. Monahan promised himself that *Just Before Dawn* would be the last horror film he would see.

He walked up the steep incline of Anderson Street into the heart of Beacon Hill. He loved the atmosphere of the place. It was straight out of a Sherlock Holmes or Jack the Ripper movie. All the narrow, winding, cobblestone streets, sumptuous brownstones, quaint shops. Boston was a great place to be for the imaginative student or artist.

Monahan didn't even mind the rain. In fact, he loved it. It added even more to the atmosphere. He could just imagine the special-effects technicians lining the tops of the sets with long watering pipes to create such an effect. Boston was so damn visual Monahan wondered why more films weren't made there.

The student peered out from under the rim of his rain hat to get a better look at the architecture. He turned left at Mount Vernon Street. He could go straight down there, recross Charles, cross the Arthur Fiedler bridge over the highway, and go right in the back way at 130 Beacon Street. On the way he could think about what sort of horror movie he would make if they gave him the money.

Monahan decided that his would be realistic. He wouldn't stick a bunch of kids out in the wilderness. He'd set the scene in any major metropolitan city. At the same time, his would be stylistic. He'd make impressionistic scenes of violence, ones that would shock as well as impress his audience.

Then he saw the blood congealing around his shoes.

John Monahan stopped dead on the sidewalk of Mount Vernon Street. He stared in wonder at the red liquid passing between his legs, carried along by a greater torrent of flowing water.

He blinked, thinking his imagination had maybe gotten the better of him. The blood was still there when he looked again. Monahan turned and followed the crimson trail back to its source. The red stuff was alternately dripping and coursing out the bottom of a drainpipe.

Monhan looked up. The pipe traveled uninterrupted all the way up to the four-story brownstone's roof. For a second, Monahan didn't know what to do. But then his imagination and curiosity got to be too much for him. He created all sorts of scenarios to explain the red liquid, some of them quite perverted and violent, but he didn't really believe any of them could actually happen. Not in real life.

Monahan was at the opposite end of the spectrum from Arlene Halliwell. She acknowledged the movies she saw as fiction but secretly felt they could be fact. Monahan was so wrapped up in the world of image-making that nothing was real anymore. Every person he met was a character. Every place he went was a set. And he couldn't leave Mount Vernon Street without checking out the possible drama at the top of the brownstone.

John Monahan trotted into the alley between the apartment houses toward the fire escape.

Judy Halliwell wasn't dead yet. She was very cold. She was on her back, her hands lying useless at her side, her mouth opening and closing like a fish out of water. The rain beat down on her as her life drooled out. She felt the hands back on her chest. They were rubbing in a circular motion. Then they were lifted and she felt a slight pressure at her waist. She heard her belt buckle being undone. She heard her zipper get pulled down. She felt the hands tugging at her waistband, trying to get the wet denim down her hips. The jeans were so tight they were taking her underwear with it.

She couldn't talk, but she could still think. She couldn't believe it. She was going to be raped while she died.

She realized it then. She was dying. She was really dying. Someone was killing her. Her head rolled to the side, some last tears mingling with the rain water on the roof.

Through her misting vision, she saw a figure appear. A man was looking at her from over the side of the building. He just seemed to be floating there, his head and shoulders above the roof line. His face held an expression of abject horror.

As she watched, she felt the hands leaving her legs. She saw another figure racing toward the man watching from over the brownstone's side. The second figure's back was dark and shapeless, disguised by a large, heavy raincoat. Incongruously, there was a thin white belt amid the tan cloth.

She saw this figure jump off the side of the building. She was surprised when it didn't fall out of sight. The two people stayed on the same level. The man fell back when

17

the other person raised a long knife. Judy watched the knife come down and go up again. Then the action was repeated. Again and again and again.

Judy Halliwell looked back up at the stars. She didn't want to see any more. Her coldness had left her. She was beginning to feel warm again. In fact, she was beginning to feel very good. Relaxed. Comfortable. Rested. She felt a strange, deep, horrible peace. A peace she knew would never end.

At the last, she remembered her Unitarian teachings. There was only the Oneness, the Unity. She was going to the God she had served so hard and so long. His beauty was far greater than anything she would find here.

Mercifully, Judy Halliwell died before her killer returned.

Chapter Two

San Francisco Homicide Inspector Harry Callahan saw *Superman II* on the cross-country plane trip. He smiled all the way through it. Not because he liked it but because he wished his own job was that easy. For a few seconds he toyed with the thought of throwing away his Magnum, ripping off his shirt, and leaping out of the 747 to fight for truth, justice, and the American way.

Then his smile and the fantasy were gone. By and large, Callahan didn't like the movie. It was beautifully done and probably very entertaining to someone who didn't get the overdoses of reality he had to deal with. Harry did not like fantasy. They were dreams and wishes that never came true. He couldn't waste his time dreaming and wishing anymore.

It was fine for someone who could pick up the morning paper, cheerily supplied by the smiling flight attendant, and read about the double murder on Beacon Hill with objective detachment. But Harry had been too close to too many murders to be detached. He had had his face rubbed in real-life murder and actual human blood. The cheery optimism of *Superman II* was not for him. When some pumped-up asshole stuck a Saturday Night Special in his face down some dark alley one night, where was Superman going to be then?

19

There would only be Harry Callahan and hundreds like him doing the best damn job they could. Under the circumstances.

Callahan didn't look up when he heard the bell. He had been on enough planes to know what it meant. They were either about to hit turbulence or about to land. Harry checked his watch. It said two o'clock P.M., California time. That meant it was three hours later Boston time. Harry had left San Francisco at nine o'clock Monday morning, supposedly the third day of his once-a-year vacation. The nationwide trip took five or six hours. The plane was due to arrive in Massachusetts at five fifteen P.M., just in time for rush hour.

"Ladies and gentlemen," came a studied, mellifluous feminine voice over the intercom, "may I have your attention please? In a few minutes we will be arriving in Boston, Massachusetts, by way of Logan Airport. Kindly return to your seats and extinguish all smoking materials. Thank you for flying us today. I hope you will think of us when you travel again. Please fasten your seat belts. . . ."

Harry waited for it: the phrase that had originated on the West Coast and spread like a fungus across the states.

"And have a nice day," the voice finished. Harry nodded. His slightly depressed irritability was capped. He didn't know anyone who didn't get at least a little surly when some plastic fantastic pulled back and let them have it with, "Have a nice day." Never had such a well-meaning bunch of words had such an adverse effect. More people kicked their dogs and chewed the heads off loved ones because of that phrase than any in Callahan's memory.

It was bad enough he had to take the vacation in the first place. Although the police force bylaws decreed it necessary, Harry had avoided the off-time as much as possible. Murderers, bless their slimy disgusting hearts, never took a day off, so Harry was usually able to sneak through his assigned off-week on the tail of an investigation.

He had been hoping his last case, the Slez murders, would last all this week as well. It seemed promising. A lawyer had killed two of his clients when it looked like he would be brought up on charges of conflict of interest, perjury, and contempt of court. He had slaved twelve years to pass the bar so he went a little overboard. The lawyer had been sly so Callahan had dug in for a long hunt. Unfortunately for Harry's plans, the lawyer had also been repentant. He had given himself up yesterday.

Harry shook his head slightly, remembering. Try as he might, he couldn't get his superior, Lieutenant Al Bressler, to assign him another case.

"The only investigating you're going to be doing," the lieutenant had informed him, "is of the coeds crawling all over Boston. Too bad they're all covered up with leggings and raincoats this time of year. They may not be California girls, but they'll have to do."

Callahan had marched fairly miserably back to his office to straighten out some paperwork and waste some time before he would force himself to go.

"Look at it this way," Bressler had suggested, following his best man back to the inspector's cubicle. "They may not be as blonde or as skimpily dressed, but there are a hell of a lot of them between the ages of eighteen and twenty-one in one place."

Harry had grunted, raising his eyebrows in mock anticipation. He typed a little, pushed some papers around, sighed, and got up to go home and pack.

As he had neared the door of Suite #750, the Homicide office in the Frisco Justice Building, Bressler had called to him a final time.

"And Harry?"

Callahan turned.

"Say hello to your folks for me."

"Not folks," Harry had corrected for the third time that week since getting the letter. "Cousins. Distant cousins."

That was the catalyst, Harry tiredly acknowledged as he stared out the plane window at Boston Harbor. A letter from his cousins on his father's side. A letter from some people he hadn't seen in more than a decade. A letter asking . . . no, begging him to come to Boston as soon as he could.

Harry held on as the plane banked in for its approach, still thinking about the letter.

"I don't want to say that it is a matter of life or death, because it is such a cliché and you probably hear that sort of thing a lot in your work, but it is. It really is a matter of great importance to us and the family. Please come. We need to talk to you. We all miss you and would like to see you very much. Love, Linda."

Linda. Linda Callahan. Harry's father had a brother. His brother had a wife who had a child. That child was Linda. Linda got married and had a child of her own. Now she was writing him, asking for some sort of help.

". . . a matter of life or death. . . ."

". . . a matter of great importance. . . ."

A "family" matter. Harry didn't want to acknowledge it. He liked to think that he didn't have a family. It hadn't always been that way. A long time ago he'd had loving parents and a beautiful bride. But they were all dead, taking whatever family feeling he once had with them.

His police job had done the rest. He had seen so much pain, so many atrocities, and so much of the underside of what love can do that he didn't want a family. He didn't want to think there were still people somewhere who could be hurt because of him. He didn't want to think there were people who could hurt him.

Still, he couldn't shut out his past. The damage had already been done. In better times he had visited his cousins, and they had taken to him. And no matter what he wanted to think they were still blood. And they had

22

written to him for help. He probably wouldn't have turned his back on a stranger in the same situation. So why did he feel so reluctant to help Linda?

Before he could find an answer, his thoughts were interrupted by the plane's final descent and the sudden, raucous sound of blaring music behind him. As soon as his ear adjusted, he realized it was the heavily over-dubbed beat of disco music. Harry pivoted in his seat, looking through the crack between chairs. Behind him was a lithe black man bopping to the beat of a huge hand-held radio-tape recorder. He had it on so loud everyone in the 747 could hear it.

The lady sitting on the aisle next to Harry was an inexperienced flier. If it wasn't her first plane trip, then it was mighty close. She had been nervous throughout the entire flight, and this final blaring noise during the craft's most crucial maneuver nearly sent her over the edge.

"Oh my God!" the matronly woman cried. "Please! Please turn that thing off."

Harry waited for the music to disappear or at least diminish in volume. It didn't happen. He saw a harried, concerned flight attendant hustle down the aisle toward him. She was obviously worried about being out of her seat during the landing procedure. She stopped behind Harry to request politely that the machine be switched off.

"Hey, baby," said the man indignantly. "You all switched off the music on the headphones, and I need the beat to keep my seat. Be cool, it's not bothering anybody."

"Its disturbing everyone," the stewardess corrected. "Would you kindly . . .!"

"No, baby," the man interrupted. "Would you kindly turn the headphones back on?"

"I can't do that."

"Then I can't do this."

Harry looked at the woman beside him. Her face was set in fear, and her knuckles were changing colors on the seat arm. The cop sighed, undoing his seat belt. He rose ominously from his chair to appear in both the black man's and stewardess' vision. Without a word he reached down, hit the "eject" button, and pulled the cassette tape out in one smooth movement.

"Hey, man, what the hell you think you're doing?" the radio man yelled.

Harry looked sympathetically at the flight attendant while casually crushing the cassette with one hand. That quieted the fellow. The stewardess smiled in thanks at Callahan and trotted back to her seat. The silence did not last long.

As they were passing over the roofs of surrounding houses to come in for the final leg of their landing, the music blared again. Harry immediately got up while turning. The black man had inserted a new tape and was looking right at Harry with a smug smile. The only difference was that he had a big black friend sitting beside him now, also with a wicked grin plastered on his mug.

Harry was unconcerned. With a fast tug, he pulled the radio out of the man's hands. The black man babbled in shock, trying to get up. The seat belt held him in for a second. While he was trying to extricate himself, Harry hit the back of the machine and neatly ripped out its six batteries. He dropped them in the black man's lap and dropped the radio in his own seat.

The black man finally undid the buckle and rose with rage. "Hey, man, you're asking. . . !"

He got those four words out before Harry grabbed the front of his shirt tightly with his right hand and lifted up. With his left hand, he hit the overhead baggage compartment release. The black man rose and the heavy hinged plastic section fell. The two objects met somewhere in the middle, the resulting crack as loud as the music had been.

Harry let go of the man's shirt front so he could fall back into his seat, eyes closed and mouth open. His friend also had his mouth open. Harry looked at him.

24

"Anything you'd like to hear?" he asked dangerously.

"No, man, oh no, sir," was what the music man's big friend said.

Harry nodded in agreement and sat down just before the 747's wheels touched ground. Along with his carry-on bag and suit holder, Harry brought the empty radio along with him as he prepared to leave the plane. As he neared the door and all the stewardesses wishing the exiting passengers a nice day, he turned to look back at the seat behind his. The big friend was still trying to awaken the music man completely. The music man was babbling incoherently, the whites of his eyes showing.

Harry turned back toward the exit just as the flight attendant he had helped approached him. She was a mature, very attractive blonde. "Thank you for your assistance," she said, slipping something into his jacket pocket. "Have a nice *night*."

Harry pulled the piece of paper out of his pocket as he walked down the airport's entry hall. It was the name, address, and room number of a Boston hotel. At the bottom of the page was a time, "11:30 on," it said, and her name, "Terri." Harry allowed himself a smile. She didn't care whether he was married, or engaged, or had a girl, or what. And to tell the truth, neither did he. Nothing ventured, nothing gained.

The San Francisco inspector walked out into the early evening of Boston. It felt like he had never left his home town. Although Boston had harder winters, the two cities were remarkably the same in late September. The air was crisp and full of the smell of the ocean. Each city was full of hills, and both had the same sort of architecture. Harry took a deep breath and walked toward a line of departing buses. He arrived just as a big, eight-wheel jobber was pulling out. As it swept into traffic, Harry nonchalantly dropped the black man's radio under the rear wheel. The machine flattened and split into a dozen unsalvageable pieces.

Harry turned to see the entire mass of humanity around the buses staring at him, tourists and redcaps alike. Harry took the moment to look up at the sky, snap his fingers, and say, "Oh darn," as if he had dropped it accidentally. Then he went over to the airline entrance to wait for Linda.

The rush hour had done its usual work. All the traffic was snarled, even on the normally well-planned airport roadways. Unless his cousin had left the house two hours early to avoid the crush, Harry was sure she'd be late. He found a concrete supporting post to lean on, set down his luggage, and contentedly watched humanity pass by.

He watched people inside the terminal wait interminately for their suitcases to crawl off the conveyor belt and onto the metal showcase. Harry glanced at his own two bags. Inside were about all the clothes he owned, really. He dressed nattily, but no one would call him a clotheshorse. Brown was his favorite color, and tweed was his favorite material. That and the regulation Levis, sport shirts, ties, and raincoat were about as far as Harry went. While the choice may have gotten boring to others, at least Harry never had to wait for his bags.

The cop redirected his gaze elsewhere. He stood on the end of a line of taxicabs, all waiting patiently for passengers they could chariot into the city and its eight sections. Harry watched the yellow cars come and go, the first in line always taking off and the others moving forward accordingly. While he waited there was only one instance of any difficulty.

Some dark-skinned foreign students were having a hard time deciding which cab they wanted to take. The driver in the head car at that time had bounded out of his seat to complain.

"Hey, you can't take the other ones. I was here first! You gotta take my cab. That's the rules. We all go in order here. That's the American way."

If ever Harry heard a cue for Superman, this was it.

But the man of steel did not show up, so Harry edged forward.

"We do not want to take your auto," the dark-skinned young man said, holding the arm of the young lady next to him. She was looking at the sidewalk, obviously confused and just a little bit scared.

"That's tough, buddy," said the cab driver. "Because either you take mine or you don't get into town."

By then Harry had sidled up to the young couple. "Where do you want to go?" he asked quietly.

The two young people turned to face the inspector. They first stared right into his chest. They weren't used to men his size. They looked up into his craggy, lined face and wind-swept, wheat-colored hair. Then they began happily babbling to each other in their native Mediterranean tongue.

"Cowboy," was the only word they said in English to each other. "Cowboy, cowboy."

Harry realized that the American film industry did more than supply the nation with superhero fantasies. It also supplied the world with visions of the United States. These two foreigners had only seen Harry's like before in Western movies. Naturally they assumed Callahan was a cowboy, too.

Once they had finally calmed, the young man was able to reply in fractured English. "We desire to travel to Cambridge."

Callahan looked over the foreigners' heads at the still-upset cabbie. "How much to Cambridge, driver?"

There was a slight pause while the driver thought. "Seven-fifty or ten dollars, depending on the traffic," the cabbie finally said.

"That is not true!" the young man exploded.

Before Harry could question the young man, the cabbie tried to roll over the foreigners with words. "What do you mean that's not true? I just said it didn't I? How do you know it's not true? You a cabbie or something? You

27

know the rates in this town? I said seven-fifty, OK? It's the best price going and if you know what is good for you, you'll take it!"

Once the driver began talking, Harry's eyes narrowed. What he had merely suspected before, he was sure of now. As the cabbie went on, Harry walked around the front of the car, approached the driver, and put one hand on the man's shoulder. The cabbie's words suddenly diminished. Harry used his other hand to put his forefinger against his lips in the "quiet" sign. The cabbie's words ran out.

"What do you mean it is not true?" Harry asked the young man from across the hood.

"He say something different to us. No seven-fifty."

Harry kept his hand on the cabbie's shoulder in a friendly manner. "What did he say to you?"

"He say that it an American custom to pay first chauffeur with all the currency in right pocket. He say it was a game of chance where if pocket were empty, one would ride free."

Harry looked at the driver like a father who has caught his son's hand in the cookie jar. His expression said, "You should have known better." The driver responded.

"They're these damn Middle-east kids," he said softly. "Iranians or Arabs or something. They've got all the oil, and they bleed us dry."

"The bleeding's got to stop somewhere," Harry told the man, then returned to the foreign pair. "How much money do you have in your right pocket?" he asked.

The young man reached slowly into his slacks and pulled out a wad as thick as a pack of tarot cards. He gave the stack of bills to Harry without hesitation. They were all fifties and twenties. Harry counted up to five hundred dollars without making a dent in the stack before stopping.

"Seven-fifty, huh?" he said to the cabbie. "More like seven hundred and fifty, wasn't it?"

The driver thought it had gone on long enough. "Hey,

28

you can't prove nothing, mister, so why don't you butt out. I've got a wife and kids to feed, y'know."

"Fine," Harry said, putting his hands up innocently. "Let's do it your way." He stuck the pile of cash in the foreigner's left pocket. "What do you have in your right pocket now?" he asked the young man. The foreigner pulled out empty cloth. "Oops," Harry said to the cabbie. "You lose."

Only then did he show the man his badge. The driver was too far away to see it was from San Francisco, and instead of checking further, he lowered his head on his taxi's roof, groaning. Harry took the opportunity to open the door for the lady.

"You make sure he takes you to the right place," he told the young man, "and if he asks for anything, call a policeman." The foreigner nodded and hopped into the back seat after his countryman. Harry returned to the driver's side. "I've got your taxi number from the trunk, and I know your name from your license inside. You give these kids any trouble, and I'll pull this car out from under you. Now go get their luggage."

Miserably, the driver did as he was told. As he prepared to get behind the wheel, Harry slapped ten dollars of his own money into the guy's hand. "For the wife and kids," he said.

The driver looked up in surprise, but Harry had already turned and walked back to his waiting spot. Callahan looked the other way as the taxi took off. It had cost him a ten-spot, but it was worth satisfying his sense of justice. Although no excuse was acceptable for the cabbie's kind of behavior, the man did have a point. Even if he had gotten away with his fraud, the kids probably wouldn't have missed the money. Their loaded daddy was sending them to the best American school, so price was no object. He had no love of the OPEC nations, but he wasn't going to blame the spoiled children for the sins of the fathers.

That set his mind back onto his own track. Blaming

the kids for the sins of their parents. It wasn't Linda's fault that his parents had died. It wasn't her fault that a drunk driver had wiped out his wife. Still, he couldn't help dreading the meeting. In the back of his mind he was sure the "life or death" matter was going to amount to something trivial. Some little personal thing that Linda had blown way out of proportion. Something she couldn't talk to anybody she knew about.

Just as he was thinking this, an orange Pinto station wagon pulled up in front of him. He groaned inwardly, guessing the occupant. Trust the car to be an orange Pinto. A Pinto, for God's sake! Who in his right mind bought a Pinto anymore?

Things lightened just a little bit as Linda stepped out of the driver's seat. She was still a handsome woman, Harry thought, as she ran around the front of the car.

"Harry!" she said happily, honestly. She practically jumped on him with a big hug. He couldn't help but be swept up in her mood. She was so visibly happy to see him, so uncloyingly delighted and pleased that he felt appreciated. He suddenly became aware that he was accepted by her. It was a strangely pleasant sensation for the hardened detective.

He returned her hug to the amused, smiling faces of the others around them. Everyone basked themselves in the feeling of family they gave off. Everybody loves a lover.

And Harry and Linda looked like a good pair. She was still young and firm with her Irish blood showing in her facial structure and her dark, almost brown, auburn hair. She wore a simple dress, but it made her appear somehow more feminine than the girls around her in pants.

She stopped hugging him but held onto his arms as she moved back for a more discerning view. "It's so good to see you again, Harry," she said without self-consciousness. "You look terrific."

Harry appraised her, the smile staying on his face. "You haven't changed," he commented.

"Oh, come on," Linda answered in disbelief, breaking away. "I'm an old lady now. Where's the rest of your bags?" She looked around the base of the concrete column.

"That's it," Harry said, motioning at the two pieces of luggage.

For the first time, real apprehension bordering on panic entered Linda's voice. It put an edge on the otherwise happy reunion scene. "You are staying the whole week?" she questioned, her voice slightly catching.

Harry didn't want to deal with it too quickly. Instead of answering her to her face, he bent down to retrieve his things. "Yeah, I just don't need much to get by," he said casually.

Linda relaxed again, and things almost went back to the way they had been. But not quite. The thing that brought him here was getting between them. They both knew it was not a social visit, and they both didn't like the idea. Linda opened the rear of the Pinto for the bags. Harry remembered the reports of rear-end collision explosions but dropped the luggage in anyway. Who was he to believe everything Geraldo Rivera said?

"It's terrible on the roads," Linda said, trying to bring the conversation back to its previous level. "Do you want to have dinner here until the rush hour ends?"

"No," Harry replied, moving to the front passenger's door. "Let's get going." He thought about the black music man and the cabbie. "Airports seem to bring out the worst in people."

Linda misunderstood. It was obvious from her subsequent silence as she threaded her way out of the Logan environs and onto the expressway into Boston. She must've thought that Harry had been referring to her with his last comment. That, or she may have thought he was irritated from waiting. Whatever the cause, she took Harry's comment to heart.

The dread that had been slightly dispelled when they met was growing again in Callahan's mind. Linda was a person he couldn't just be with. She was blood. He felt an obligation to deal with her. To work around her moods. To play all the obligation games that relatives were expected to play. Even though he hated the idea, he still couldn't bring himself to find out the specifies of what Linda wanted.

As they crossed the expressway bridge and Boston rose in the sunsetted distance, Harry looked out the window at the *U.S.S. Constitution,* the revolutionary war frigate anchored in the Boston Navy Yard. "Old Ironsides" was its nickname, and it heralded travelers to their first view of Boston's historic heritage.

Callahan wasn't much interested in sightseeing. He also wasn't much interested in family affairs. He mentally steeled himself for a long week.

"How's Peter?" he asked, breaking silence's grip on the car.

"All right, I guess," Linda responded, her sudden dourness as much attributable to the snarled traffic as Harry's attitude. "He's not working as much as he'd like. You know, with inflation and recession and everything."

Harry nodded. He remembered the Peter Donovan he had met at the wedding a little more than twenty years ago. They were both about the same age then, young and full of hope. Harry had only talked to the groom a little bit, but he liked the man. He'd make a good hunting and drinking buddy. But that was years ago when Harry did a lot more drinking and a lot less hunting.

"Still in construction?" he asked as a follow-up. That's me, he thought, Harry Callahan, master interrogator.

"Yes," Linda answered simply. She paused, then thought it was worth more of a reply. "Almost finished an apartment house in Revere. Funds ran out. He's waiting for the backers to come up with more." Linda didn't like the way that sounded. It made her depressed. She changed the subject. "How're you doing?"

"I keep busy," Harry answered, not particularly wanting to go into detail.

"We read about you sometimes in the paper," Linda spoke up, her voice getting perky again. "A couple of years ago when you saved the governor from those terrorists on Riker's Island."

Harry didn't like to think about that either. It seemed that most of his memories involved losing something close, or at least getting close, to him. He had lost Inspector Kate Moore on that case. She was his one and only female partner. He had liked her more than just as a police associate. She was killed by a terrorist before Harry managed to blow her murderer to kingdom come.

No, he didn't like to think about it. But since the subject had already been brought up, he figured Linda might as well have her facts right.

"It was the mayor, not the governor," he told her, still looking out the window. "And it was at Alcatraz. Riker's Island is in New York."

Linda's voice went back to its dull level. "Oh. Sorry."

"No problem," said Harry. He turned to her, getting a little tired of the Harold Pinter play being enacted inside the car. "What's this section of town?" he asked, referring to the heavily business-oriented buildings that were cropping up around them.

"Oh," Linda livened, "this is Back Bay. It neighbors and incorporates the Italian North End, Government Center, which is right over there, and beyond that, Beacon Hill."

"Beacon Hill?" he echoed. "Is that where those murders were?"

That would do the trick, Harry thought smugly. If there was one thing housewives in orange Pintos liked to talk about, it was juicy murders. Callahan had discovered that from experience. During his office's once-a-year open house for the public, he was consistently amazed by the continual flow of meek, unassuming men and women who wanted to talk about nothing but the most excruciatingly detailed murders.

Linda surprised him. He had badly misjudged her. His own discomfort and reluctance had affected his opinion of her. Instead of answering immediately, she approached the subject delicately. "Yes," she said very quietly, almost in a whisper. "A college boy and a . . . a young girl. It was horrible," she finished with a rush of breath. Then she started to cry.

Harry's hand went to the wheel as the car began to crawl into another lane. Linda tried to control her emotions but could not. The tears rolled out faster, and she began to shake uncontrollably. As her foot fell off the accelerator, the car slowed.

Visions of the vehicle turning into a firebomb pushed Harry into action. He was pulling the wheel back, kicking out for the pedals and spinning around to look behind at the same time.

The Pinto swerved back into the middle lane as a Cutlass Supreme zoomed up behind them. A second vision of a rush-hour pile-up got Harry moving faster. He reached over and hit the right turn signal. His shoe pushed Linda's foot out of the way and pressed down on the accelerator. He turned his eyes front to spot an exit up ahead. The car to their right had braked a bit when they first began to sneak over, so when Harry speeded up, it drifted farther behind. There was just enough room to squeeze between it and the car ahead of them.

Harry took the chance, pulling the steering wheel hard to the right. The Pinto responded surprisingly well. It practically jumped right to the side, scraping off only a coat of paint in the process as it screeched in between the other autos. Harry kept the wheel down, pulling even more with his other hand. The Ford turned even farther, just missing the embankment and careening down the exit ramp.

A car behind them, having already turned to exit, had to slam on its brakes to avoid rear-ending them on the ramp. The word "PINTO" in metal on the hatch-back did much to help. Thankfully, there was no one else right

34

behind the car right behind them. Harry had avoided a pile-up on the highway and on the exit ramp.

He managed to keep the car straight and even braked at the bottom of the exit road. "Linda," he said. "Come on, snap out of it." His cousin didn't seem to hear. She was wrapped up in her own world of tragedy. Real or imagined, Harry didn't know yet.

The car behind them blew its horn, so Harry had no choice but to continue driving from the passenger's side. He looked up at the myriad roads and signs in front of him. It was the most incredible mess he had ever seen except in Manhattan. And even there, the confusion came from too many cars, no lanes, and potholes. Here, the roads were well-groomed but totally chaotic. They twisted and turned in every direction, and more cars came from every other direction.

As far as he could tell, Callahan couldn't go right or straight. From the signs and traffic flow, it seemed he could go left, bear to the left, bear slightly to the right, or turn all the way around. He settled on taking close to a U-turn, since all these angry-looking grillworks were bearing down on him from every other roadway.

He pulled the steering wheel all the way to the right as if he were hauling in a line, hand over hand. The car turned in a tight radius and wound up going parallel to the expressway in the opposite direction. Harry saw they were heading toward some empty-looking warehouses. He saw a few other cars parked along what looked like an alleyway.

He pulled alongside these parked cars in front of some boarded-up shops. The smell of decaying fat was everywhere. As he pulled himself back to his seat, away from his blubbering cousin, he saw the quaint wooden shops flanked by a large office building on one side, an empty, glass-strewn lot on the other, and a system of highway ramps on the third side.

The little orange Pinto stalled in the barren oasis just a few hundred feet from the frenzied activity behind Government Center. Linda was finally able to make sense again as night drew in on Boston.

"Harry," she sobbed. "I knew that girl. I saw her all the time with Shanna."

Shanna was her daughter. As soon as her name was mentioned, Harry pictured her in his mind. She was a bonnie little Irish lass of ten with a warm, cheery face that wasn't quite round and wasn't quite sharp. Her lips were little things but amazingly expressive. Her hair was bright red, and freckles covered every square inch of her skin.

Harry saw her as he remembered her. Facing his big, unsmiling form without fear. Looking at his already lined face and gnarled hands, she sized him up and named him on the spot, "Uncle Harry." His rough demeanor hadn't fooled her for a second. They used to play together. She had made him wish that his wife would give him a daughter.

Then his wife had died, and the wishes had gone all away unanswered. Harry's vision of Shanna misted and was swept away by the realization that she was twenty years old now. No longer a little girl playing with her kind, sensitive Uncle Harry. A lot of things had changed inside the cop since then. He wondered if his rough exterior could fool her now. It fooled everybody else in the world. Even himself.

Slowly, he became aware of Linda again. She was still speaking between tears. "They both did volunteer work for the Unitarian Church. Oh God, Harry, I'm so afraid Shanna will be next."

Chapter Three

Murder. Just like any other city, Boston was no stranger to it. In fact, Boston was the site of one of the more infamous mass-murder sprees in modern history. Not even Son of Sam, the man who made the .44 famous, had the far-reaching fame and reputation of the Boston Strangler. But then again, Son of Sam was not played by Tony Curtis in a big-grossing movie.

Funny, Harry thought as he walked through Scollay Square, the section that was generally known as Government Center. Albert DeSalvo, the alleged, and now dead, perpetrator of the Strangler crimes was the first of the modern waves of men who killed for no other reason than to simply kill. The Strangler and Richard Speck had paved the way for such more recent notables as the Hillside Strangler and Charles Manson. Manson had done the world a further disservice by murdering a movie star. The papers had made so much of it that the madman and his sick clan had become media stars themselves. A motion picture for television was made from a best-selling book, both named after the song title Manson had scrawled on the wall of the slaughterhouse. And the tragedy had come full circle. Another media murder star was made when the co-writer of that song Manson found so inspirational was murdered in New York.

Harry felt just a little bit sick. If he hadn't known so

much about death already, he would have been surprised that such a peaceful, handsome city could have been a part of such hate and waste. It was sad and frightening at the same time, Harry decided as he neared the edge of the $100,000,000 Plaza.

There was a multitiered fountain and an apartment house to his right. There was the Town Hall behind him. There was a shopping center and an office building across the street. To his left was a coffeehouse with a big, steaming teakettle hanging above the door.

Harry remembered Linda's directions. He went past the coffeehouse and up Tremont Street. He passed a few restaurants, a hotel, and a cheese shop. He passed a movie theater, a recruiting center, and a cemetery. All were crammed into one short, curving block. He stepped out onto the northeast corner of the Boston Common.

Stretched out in front of him was a huge patch of wooded grassland, a park that covered the area of two square city blocks, framed by Tremont and Beacon streets with Charles Street passing through the middle.

"Take a right and walk up to the Gold Dome," Linda had said. The Gold Dome was the top of the Massachusetts Statehouse, Harry remembered. Right next to it was the Unitarian Headquarters—where Shanna was supposed to be.

Harry watched the many people going home from work and from school across the huge tree-covered plain in the evening gloom. He saw businessmen in three piece suits. He saw teenagers in jeans and sweaters. He saw old women feeding the pigeons and young women walking their dogs. There were some kids playing baseball in the fenced-off lot near the corner of Tremont and Charles Streets. He saw lovers walking, holding hands. He saw old men reading newspapers on the benches around the old-fashioned gazebo in the middle of the park.

Anyone else could've surveyed this sunset-dappled scene and thought about the grace, nobility, and great variety of the human species. All Harry could think about was murder. He saw the passersby and knew murder could come to or from any one of them. And for no reason. He remembered the *Perry Mason* TV show. He remembered the actor Raymond Burr cross-examining the suspect until he or she broke down and admitted to the killing. More importantly, they admitted why they killed.

That was the end of an era. Like it or not, television and movies influenced people. Most of the people Harry hauled in usually confessed to their inspirations: "She cheated on me. . . ." "He tried to ruin me. . . ."

More recently, Harry remembered a premiere episode of *Charlie's Angels* his associate and sometime partner Frank DiGeorgio had made him watch one night. The actor Jack Albertson had played a crazy man who took photos of models until he thought he knew enough about them to kill them. When the girls finally ran him to ground—because of a coincidence, not detective work—he told him his motive.

"I don't know," he said. "I don't know."

That was the primary cause of violent death today, Harry thought sardonically. More and more he was capturing killers who couldn't care less why they killed. "I didn't like his face. . . ." "I felt like it. . . ."

The words of the girl who had opened up with a rifle on a grammar school playground came back to him. "I don't like Mondays." Terrific. Harry knew some people who didn't like any day of the week.

Harry looked away from the Common and concentrated on the steep incline of the wide sidewalk he was traversing. He felt the comforting weight of his Smith and Wesson Model 29 .44-caliber Magnum in its shoulder holster, and he was glad he had it. He couldn't remember where he heard it, but he still felt the line had the solid basis of truth. "An armed society is a polite society."

The San Francisco inspector emptied his mind of the dour thoughts. It must be jet lag, Harry reasoned about his depressive state of mind. That, or he was fighting

39

against the feeling that he still cared. He had always known that he cared for some things. Things like justice. But he hadn't felt like he cared for some body for years. There were people he was concerned about, people he liked and had faith in, but no one he really let himself care for. He already knew full well the dangers in caring. Then Shanna had to enter his life again.

Linda had said that her daughter was confused. She was trying to "find herself" almost any way she could. She was striking off in all directions at once, trying to find a suitable solution to "who she was." Linda thought she was making some mistakes along the way.

That was mother talk, Harry decided. He translated to himself that Shanna was going too fast, weaving across too many lanes for her own good. She was trying things that she shouldn't simply for the sake of experience. On the plus side, she was helping at the Unitarian Headquarters in many capacities. On the minus side, she was discovering new means of worship from other people there.

"It is some sort of Fellowship group unconnected to the church," Linda had said. "Shanna says it's based on many American Indian precepts of honor. But all I know, Harry, is that she comes over late at night sometimes and doesn't know who she is. We sit in the kitchen and talk about the strangest things, and she doesn't know who she is. And the scary thing is she doesn't care.

"I try to keep her there until she remembers her name, but she still usually goes back to her apartment. One night though, she slept over. We still keep her room available. So I took her clothes to the laundry room downstairs. They were a mess. Her nice blue skirt and a white shirt. There were brown and deep red spots all over the shirt, Harry. I'm sure they were bloodstains."

Callahan stopped in front of the Unitarian Headquarters. He had come to the end of the block along the north side of the Common. He had crossed the street in front of the gold-topped Statehouse. The building right next door, to the left as you looked at it, was the Unitarian facilities.

It was a big, multistoried place of handsome design. There was a small portico and stone stairway up to a handsome wood door. On the second floor was a large window made up of many small panes of clear, bright glass that almost looked like crystal. On either side of this window were several hanging flags. One was the American flag, one was the Massachusetts state flag, and the last was the Unitarian flag.

Farther down the street were more handsome buildings looking out onto the west side of the Common. Harry trotted up the stone steps and tried the door. It was unlocked. He opened it onto a handsome wood hall with an office to the right—connected by a box-office-like window to the foyer—a wide stairway up on the left, and a lobby in front of him.

It was after working hours so the office and lobby were empty. But there were still signs of activity upstairs. Harry did not stand on ceremony. He walked right up the steps, keeping his eyes and ears open. He heard a boisterous discussion coming from somewhere above him. At first he couldn't make out the words. They were just loud and obviously spoken by a male. The higher he climbed, the clearer the words became.

"You don't understand . . .," he heard at first.

"Don't worry . . . complete control. . . ." Harry became aware of some soft mumbles in between the male ragings. It sounded as if a girl and boy were talking—the girl being the calm one in the situation.

"I tell you no!" the male voice shouted. "You can't! I won't let you! Who is the boss here anyway?"

The words were coming from a single doorway near the front of the building on the second floor. When Harry reached the top of the stairs he could begin to hear both sides of the conversation.

"I don't like it," said a quiet female voice. "It isn't fun anymore."

"It's not supposed to be fun!" the angry male replied. "We are supposed to stand for something. We're supposed to be working toward something. We need everyone's energy, everyone's manitou to keep our power up!"

"Come on, Tom, there's no reason to come down so hard," said a third voice, another female.

"I'm only thinking about what we're trying to achieve!" the newly christened Tom said. "We can't afford to lose anybody now. We can't!"

"Tom, you're raving," said the first female's calm voice. "Have you eaten today?"

"I'm on a fast," Tom answered sullenly.

"You're on a strike," the woman answered. "You haven't eaten for days. You've hardly slept. . . ."

"You know why! You know why!" Tom replied, his hysteria reaching a peak.

"Come on, Tom, take it easy," said the third voice.

"Yeah, hey, I don't know about you," the first girl said soothingly, "but I'm starving. Tell you what, Tom. Why don't we talk this over some more at Brigham's or the Muffin House or something?"

"I'm not going to eat!" the boy yelled. "I have to see the wolf!"

"All right, OK," the first girl soothed. "But you can watch me eat, can't you? That won't scare the wolf away, will it?"

"Don't scoff, Christine," the boy said threateningly. "I'm warning you. . . ."

Harry had heard enough. His sense of timing told him it was a good moment for making himself known. He walked over and leaned against the doorway.

All three people inside froze in place. They were standing in what looked like a loft—a wide, fairly high enclosure that consisted of one room interrupted only by round support beams. The only window in the large space was a big one made to look like an arc in the far wall. Through it Harry could see most of the Common. Around the room were tables covered with pamphlets and boxes of

42

envelopes. On the corner of the farthest table was a typewriter and several stamp dispensers.

Behind the tables were the trio of young people. The boy was very good-looking. He was tall, brown-haired, well built, and wearing a tight sweater, designer jeans, and boots. The girl next to him was a knockout. She could've been any age between eighteen and twenty-seven. She had loosely curled brown hair that rolled lustrously down to her shoulders and broiled over her forehead. Her eyes were perfectly shaped and deep brown. Her lips were inordinately rich and red. She looked to be model height —about five-nine. All her feminine parts hung onto her for dear life.

She too was wearing jeans but had a beige, silky-looking shirt tucked into them. Her lines were smooth, shaped, and strong. Callahan was impressed. Compared to the tan blondes of California, this rich-skinned brunette gave off a solid glow to their pale yellow rays.

Shanna was behind her. There was no mistaking her. The hair was still bright red, but it was longer and parted slightly to the side. The freckles were still there, blasting into every corner of her face. From a distance they combined to give her normally pretty pale skin color the impression of a tan. Her eyes were bright green and her lips, still fairly thin, were highlighted with lipstick. She was wearing a blue leotard top and jeans. Shanna's denims were worn and obviously non-fashion Levis, Lees, or Wranglers. The brunette's jeans were obviously designer, Vanderbilts or Calvin Kleins or Sergio Valentes or one of those thirty-four million other labels.

Taken together, the two women could make a weaker man fall to his knees and beg to kiss the ground they walked on.

The recognition was instantaneous on Shanna's part as well. Her eyes widened. Christine's eyes looked him over with pleased appraisal. Tom's eyes couldn't help but stay the way they were: bloodshot, heavily lined, and slightly bulging.

"Harry," Shanna breathed.

The other two looked at her at the same time.

"You know him?" Christine asked.

"He's my uncle . . . I mean, a relative of mine," Shanna hastily corrected herself.

"Good Heavens," Christine replied, turning back to Harry. "Where have you been hiding him?"

Tom interrupted in the same suave manner he had been handling the rest of the conversation with. "How long have you been out there?" he demanded in a voice that neared rage.

"I just came in," Harry answered quietly.

"That doesn't answer my question!" Tom yelled.

Harry shrugged. "It'll have to do."

Tom's hands were clenching and unclenching. He started to move toward Callahan.

"Tom," Shanna called out, "take it easy. He's a cop."

Tom froze again. He looked frightened for a second, then closed down on all expression. His face became a calm blank slate.

"What are you doing here, Harry?" Shanna asked.

"I was in the neighborhood so I thought I'd drop in. Would you buy that?"

Shanna's expression said that she wouldn't. First she smirked because of the hoary cliché, then she thought about why Callahan would actually be there. She turned sullen, looking down.

Christine took it all in. "Well," she said lightly. "I guess you two have a lot to talk about." One good cliché deserves another, Harry thought. "I'm ready for a little supper anyway. Coming, Tom?"

"Yeah, right," said the young man flatly.

Christine went out first. Harry entered the room so she could get out the doorway without rubbing him down. She looked disappointed about the missed opportunity. As she exited she favored him with a smile that said "Hello, welcome to Boston" at the very least and "I'd like to see you in a *Playgirl* photo spread" at the very most.

Harry had to admit to himself that he wouldn't mind doing an extended stake-out on her either. And if Di-Georgio ever came into the office with pictures of her in *Playboy*, he wouldn't keep himself from folding her out.

Tom gave him a look as he left after Christine that would only fit in *Field and Stream*. Harry could even smell his lack of nutriments on his breath. When he passed, the air had a definite aroma of rotting liver.

Shanna waited until the door downstairs slammed shut. "It's Mom, right?" she said, still looking at the table and fingering the corner of a brochure.

Harry moved farther into the room. "I had the vacation time coming," he said. "I thought I'd visit." She still didn't look up. Harry stopped on the other side of the table from her. "It's been a long time," he said.

She looked up then. Her green eyes were clear and close to devastating. Her lips were set. She nodded curtly. "A long time," she agreed.

They looked at each other for a while. Harry could see Shanna mentally arguing with herself. He could imagine she hated her mother for sicking Harry on her, but she had too many fond memories of him to completely reject him. All the pent-up anger and indignity was going to be unleashed on Linda the next time mother and daughter met.

Finally, Shanna looked down again, her index fingers making little circles atop a pamphlet. "I heard about your wife," she said. "I'm sorry."

"Me, too," said Harry simply.

"I mean I'm sorry we didn't come to the funeral."

"You were too young. You lived too far away. It was ten years ago. It's over. Don't worry about it."

"A lot has changed since then," Shanna continued, building up assurance. "I'm not a little girl anymore."

"Obviously," Harry commented.

Shanna looked down at herself. She saw the solid musculature, the wide, strong breasts, and the long legs. She looked at Harry with a smile. She wasn't insulted. He had said it in a non-sexual manner. "I'm pretty together," she said with a combination of humor and conviction.

Harry figured it was a good time to introduce a more delicate subject matter. He wanted to find out more about her blackouts and bloodstains. "Linda says you're pretty popular, all right."

The chill returned between them. "What does she know?" Shanna said vindictively. "I don't even live there anymore." The redhead started busying herself with the envelopes and stamps.

Harry didn't let up. "But you visit occasionally. And you talk."

"What is this? The third degree?" Shanna wondered, trying to make it sound funny, but her voice cracked just a bit.

"Come on, Shanna, you know better than that. I'm just concerned, that's all. I want to know how you are."

"No, I don't know!" Shanna flared, the Irish temper coming into evidence. "It was ten years ago, Harry. We don't play anymore. I'm not that little girl anymore. I've changed. I've changed inside."

"So have I," Harry interjected softly.

"Hey," Shanna went on, unabated, "if anybody should know better, it's you! Where do you come off coming in here and trying to question me? It may look the same, Harry, but this isn't San Francisco. You've got no jurisdiction here. So back off, copper. You wanted to see how I was? So you saw me. I'm fine. I'm taking care of my own life. You can go back to Mom and tell her that. Then you can go back west!"

Harry bore the tirade out in silence. Questions weren't answered, but under the tongue-lashing Harry was ready to tell himself that Shanna was right. It was none of his business. Linda could've been wrong. The supposed bloodstains could've been ink, they could've been chocolate, they could've been anything. Shanna could've just been exhausted and uncommunicative after a long night. Harry was ready to accept all of it as a mother's imagination when he glimpsed something over Shanna's shoulder.

As she yelled at him, he saw Tom and Christine running across the Common. Even in the twilight and even from that distance, Harry could see it wasn't the playful run of laughing friends. Christine was running from Tom. As Harry watched, Tom caught up with her and slapped her across the back. The girl fell down, and Tom fell on top of her. They became a fuzzy jumble, but Harry could tell that an arm was rising and falling quickly, curtly, violently.

By the time he reconcentrated on Shanna, she was a bit remorseful over her outburst. "Look, Harry," she said miserably. "It is good to see you. Why don't we start again? Look, I'm not doing anything after I finish here. Why don't we go to eat someplace? Just talk and catch up with what is going on with each other?"

Harry pulled her face into focus after trying to make out the two others' struggling forms again. "I'll be right back," he said, not really hearing her offer. "Hang on," he said more to Christine than to Shanna. "I'll be right there." With that he was out the door and running down the stairs.

Callahan barreled through the office's front door and out into the four lanes of Beacon Street. Cars coming around the corners braked madly to avoid the tall man who raced right out into the street. Harry dodged behind one swerving car. The other braked right in front of him. He leaped without slowing down and ran across its still bucking hood. He outran two other cars and went through an ornate entrance gate on the side of the park. He ran down a long, multileveled stone stairway flanked by lion sculptures into the park. He watched the faraway forms of Christine and Tom as he went. The boy had sat up. The girl was cowering flat out beneath him. He was yelling something at her while punching her across the body.

As Harry neared, he saw Tom pull something out of

his waistband. He saw what it was and heard what he was shouting at the same time.

It was a hunting knife. A long, sharp, carved-handle hunting knife. Tom swept back and forth viciously in front of Christine's terrified face.

"You want it?" he shouted. "You want it? I'll give it to you, by God! You're asking for it!"

The Magnum was out and in his hand almost before Harry knew it. He pointed it up in the air and pulled the trigger. The resounding boom turned heads across the length of eight city blocks. All the birds resting in trees nearby took off, darkening the night sky even more. Harry didn't care. He had fired the gun to serve one purpose. It worked. He got Tom's attention.

Both the young man and Christine had stiffened at the loud report. Tom whirled to see Harry running at him. He leaped off the girl's body and charged in the opposite direction. Harry slowed when he neared the brunette. She was slightly bruised and her clothes were scuffed, but other than that she looked all right. Harry had to make sure before he continued.

"Are you all right?" he called as he neared.

She gulped a few times, sat up with her hands flat on the ground, and replied, "Yes, I think so."

"Go back to the church," Harry said, picking up speed. "Stay there. I'll be back." Then he sped by, going right after Tom.

The young man tore across the way, passing the gazebo and sending another squadron of birds into the air. They rose lazily and drifted back down just as Harry charged through the same location, scattering them again.

Callahan could see some brightly lit stores through the trees. He could see a parking garage, a clothes store, a Dunkin' Donuts, and the Muffin House Christine had mentioned before. Next to that was a large movie-theater marquee. Tom was heading right for it.

Atop the marquee it said "A Sack Theater," and below that the legend, "The Savoy I & II." Tom charged across the street, narrowly missing a few screeching cars himself, and right inside the place. Harry took the moment the cars had stopped to shift into fourth and followed in Tom's wake before the traffic started moving again.

As he ran past, Harry saw that the box office out front was closed. Pulling open the glass door he charged into a long hallway lined with movie posters, which ended in another set of doors. Surprisingly, they didn't lead to the theater, they emptied out into an alleyway.

Harry stopped in that street for a second. Across the narrow way was another set of doors and another box office. He looked down both sides of the alley for any sign of Tom. He was nowhere to be seen. Harry ran to the second set of doors. He saw Tom trying to elbow through two burly ushers to get in a side door along the hall.

The cop ripped open the door in front of him and roared down the red-carpeted hall, his gun still out. The ushers leaped into the theater and ran into the men's room. Tom had wanted to go through the theater and out the exit doors, but that plan was ruined by Harry's appearance. Instead he ran farther down the wide, well-lit hall.

The movie posters were getting bigger and bigger as Harry went farther and farther. Suddenly to his left a much larger theater appeared, its lobby rising two stories and a big chandelier hanging from the high ceiling. It was one of Boston's classic old theaters turned into one of the last of the movie palaces. Tom seemed unconcerned. He raced right by it and out the rear doors to another street. Harry saw him go right and quickly followed.

The cop raced out and stopped dead in the middle of a thin, heavily traveled back street. Dozens of shoppers scattered when they saw his gun still clutched in his right hand. But look as he might, Harry could no longer spot the young man.

Cautiously, Harry put his gun away and went right. Next door to the Savoy was another theater, the Paramount. But it had fallen on harder times. It was locked up tight, its last attraction being a porno flick, the posters of which were still gathering dirt along the wall. The only thing between the theaters was a snack bar. Its doors were open. Harry looked inside.

The room was large and long, stretching back hundreds of feet. Beyond the relatively small soda fountain was what Harry used to call a penny arcade, but what they now were calling a "family amusement center." Inside he could see the flashing lights and hear weird sounds of pinball and video machines. He also heard the raucous noise of disco music, badly amplified.

Slowly, Harry entered. There was a three-step stairway to his right, leading up to a platform lined with pinball machines. Harry stepped up, moving down the line while keeping an eye out along the path he had just left. Everytime he passed another machine he'd glance at the back of the person playing it. No one fit Tom's description.

He stepped down at the end of the line. It, in turn, led into a larger room filled with machines. Along each wall was another line of pinball devices. Taking up every available space in the middle of the floor were video machines, air-hockey games, and pool tables. Harry began to scan the area closely for any sign of Tom. He was about to back out and check somewhere else when his eyes settled on a face and form he recognized.

The form was of another radio-tape recorder. The face was that of the music man's big friend. As he watched, the big black dude elbowed another man lining up a billiard shot next to him.

"Hey, what the fuck you doin', my man," the shooter complained, turning. "Can't you see I'm setting up a shot?" The shooter was the music man. He stopped wailing when he saw Harry.

"Well, well, well!" he said, exhaling mightily. "Look who we have here! Hey, boys," he called. A bunch of big black dudes made themselves seen all around the pool

50

table. Harry counted five in all, counting the gloating music man.

"Remember the honkie I told you about on the plane?" the music man asked rhetorically.

"Yeah, Jack," said the big friend. "The one who smashed your ghetto blaster."

"One and the same," the music man smiled, motioning at Harry with his cue stick.

The other men started picking up cue sticks and billiard balls. "Well," said one. "We got to teach the whitey that it's not nice to break other people's property."

"Yeah, Jack," said another. "A honkey could get hurt that way."

They all started to move in on him. Harry faced them without concern. When he figured that they had gone far enough, he pulled out the Magnum and leveled it at them.

The group of stalking blacks became a shocked tableau. Everyone froze in place. Even without its hammer cocked, the .44 Magnum was a marvelous weapon for intimidation. One could look down the barrel and see his life go past in Cinerama.

"I see you haven't learned *your* lesson yet," Harry said to the music man. "Still buying and playing those things in public places."

"You want me to turn it off?" the black man said politely. "I will. I really will." He turned to switch the machine off.

"Hold it!" Harry ordered. "Any of you see a white kid come in here? About six-one, brown hair, wearing . . . !"

That was as far as Callahan got. Tom came tearing out from behind the air-hockey machine to Harry's side. Harry was pacing him by turning with the Magnum pointed even before the boy had gone three steps. The boy had almost made it to the fountain when Harry opened his mouth to shout "Halt!"

He didn't get that far. He had made a simple mistake.

51

He had turned his back on the black gang. A cue stick was smashed across his shoulders from behind.

Harry fell forward, the gun clattering out of his grip. He saw it fall under a fountain chair as he slid past on the tile floor. He ignored the pain in his back as he threw himself even harder at Tom. The boy had tried to run again when Harry was hit, but he had only made it to the door when Callahan grabbed his leg. Harry threw him down as he got up.

The cop looked back at the fountain. The music man was running toward his gun while the rest of the guys bore down on Harry. Callahan reacted immediately. He gripped Tom by the back of the collar and waistband. He anchored his feet and heaved. The groggy kid catapulted up and into the quartet of blacks.

Harry was right behind the young honkie. As two Negroes were knocked over and the other pair pushed back, Harry swung at the man nearest the fountain. His fist connected soldly, and the black dropped, his head bouncing off the edge of the counter. While the other standing man tried to get around the three struggling bodies on the floor, Harry went after the music man.

The black had just gotten his fingers around the Magnum grip when Harry kicked him in the jaw. Since the black's head was below the lip of the counter, he rose fast, smashed the back of his head into it hard, and dropped like a cement block.

The Magnum wasn't so lucky. It fell backward out of the music man's hand, arched through the air, and landed on the pool table behind the still blaring radio. The other black finally reached Harry, trying to get him in a full nelson. Harry jerked him backward into the counter lip, effectively smashing the man's kidneys with the Formica slab. That broke the grip. Harry spun and kneed him between the legs.

The man doubled over. Harry grabbed his belt and threw him into the two other Negroes who were trying to get up. They all went down again, but Tom managed to slither out from underneath. The young man stumbled to his feet and dove toward the gun on the pool table. Harry followed right behind.

Just as Tom got his hands on the Magnum, Harry grabbed the ghetto blaster. Tom turned around, pointing the weapon as Harry brought the radio resoundingly down on top of the kid's head.

Tom dove forward like Mark Spitz on a good day. He fell face first on the tile, the Magnum clattering next to him. The machine in Harry's hand sputtered and died.

The music man's friend came roaring up and out of the black pile while the other men just struggled to stand. Harry met the big black halfway, pulling the broken radio around in a wide arc. The big black practically stuck his face right into it. The radio split apart in tens of tiny spinning pieces. The man's face seemed to vibrate in flesh waves from the shock, then his eyes closed and he flew sideways right on top of a pinball machine. He crashed through the glass top, and the scoring mechanism went crazy.

Harry slowly retrieved his Magnum and straightened to face the last pair of blacks. They stared at him as if he were a whole army of Ku Klux Klan members.

"Bingo," Harry said. They must have thought he said "Boo!" because they nearly knocked each other over again trying to get out the exit door at the same time.

Harry tiredly picked up Tom, dragged him over to the soda fountain, and asked the wide-eyed man behind the counter directions to the nearest police station.

Chapter Four

"I can't help you. You'll have to wait for Detective Collins."

It was the fourth time Harry had heard that. A guy can't make a dollar with any ease in this town, Harry thought. All he wanted to do was book Tom and then get him alone in a room for a little talk. That wasn't too much to ask, was it? The Boston Police Department could extend that little courtesy for a visiting inspector, couldn't they?

It certainly didn't seem that way. First, Tom had screamed excessive violence—"police brutality" in the lingo of the sixties—and demanded medical care. When the police doctor had only found a bump on his head and no horrible wound with an accompanying concussion, Tom had screamed for his rights, his phone call, and the name of a good lawyer.

The friendly, mostly chubby, and seemingly agreeable cops had kept Tom on ice for a few hours now, occupying him with pictures and prints, the arrest report, and other delightful official things like that. In the meantime, they also entertained Harry by getting his statement. When they heard about the Unitarian Church offices and the hunting knife, they hastily got together for a huddle and then called downtown.

Ever since, Harry had felt trapped in a Samuel Beckett-like play that might have been titled *Waiting for Detective Collins.*

The police station was very familiar. It was like many other municipal police stations in that it was housed in one of the city's oldest buildings. But rather than being rundown and corroded, Boston's station house was a solid stone structure just a couple of blocks away from the theater section and Boston College.

It was after ten o'clock in the evening when Detective Collins finally arrived. He swept into the squad room, his furry tan coat unbelted and unbuttoned off a nice pinstripe suit. Detective Collins was well dressed, well groomed, good-looking, and as black as the boys Harry had beaten up at the pinball emporium.

"Detective Christopher Collins," a woman sergeant introduced, after bringing the man over to where Harry sat, "Inspector Harry Callahan of the San Francisco Homicide Department."

Collins' handshake was solid and warm. "It getting boring on the West Coast, Inspector?" Collins said as way of hello. "You trying to solve all our murders, too?"

Harry stood. Collins was a couple of inches shorter than he was. About five-eleven or six feet, Harry judged. "Just happened to be at the wrong place at the right time," Harry replied.

Collins looked beyond Harry at the collected arrest reports on the desk. "We'll see," he murmured, scanning them. He turned to the sergeant, who looked like a retired librarian. "I'm glad you called me." He then straightened, started to walk out of the room, and motioned for Harry to follow. Harry left the harried, forever active squad room to their work. He caught up to Collins in the hall. The black cop was still studying the reports.

"I've been assigned to the Beacon Hill Murders that happened last night," Collins explained. "Some things you say in here look like they could be connected with it."

"I figured as much," said Harry, glancing around the hall as they went. "Both the murder victim and the attacked girl worked at the Unitarian Church, and both were attacked with knives."

"Hmmph," Collins grunted, eyes still on the papers in front of him as he seemingly walked around by radar. "Christine, huh? Is that the only name you know for her?"

"We weren't properly introduced. I could find out. Call the Unitarian offices. She might still be there."

"We have," said Collins. "She wasn't." Harry nodded, unsurprised. "No problem, though," Collins continued. "We will call in the morning. Anyone on duty there will know her full name."

The black detective looked at Callahan out the corner of his eye. Harry saw it with his own peripheral vision but acted as if he hadn't. It was an old, tired trick. Always try to put the other person on guard; always act if the other person has something to hide.

It often worked because almost everybody who walked into a police station without a badge had something to hide. Whether they were reporting a crime, the victim of one, or the perpetrator, everyone had the feeling that the cops wanted to know every single detail of their lives. In actuality, they were probably right.

Harry certainly knew that he was hiding something. He had failed to mention Shanna's involvement with the girl, Shanna's shared conversation with the two, or even that Shanna existed. According to his statement, Harry had been just passing by when he saw the two young people go running out of the Unitarian Headquarters.

It was a calculated gamble. Shanna's father's name was Donovan. If Collins was to think Harry had relatives in the city he'd find no directly related Callahans. If Collins found one of the drivers who just missed Harry on Beacon Street, he could prove him as a liar, but that was doubtful. As it stood, only Shanna and Harry knew the truth. And Collins didn't know about Shanna, and Harry wasn't talking.

So Callahan ignored the questioning silence and Collins' suspicious glance. He saw no reason to bring his relatives into it at this point, especially since the "alleged perpetrator" was in custody. "Where are we going now?" Harry inquired easily.

"Your wish is my command," said Collins. "We're going to pay Tom Morrisson a little visit."

The interrogation-detention room was remarkably like all the others Harry had visited in his career. Then again, you could take any room and line every inch of wall space with cork and get the same look. White corkboard was everywhere. Within its pristine confines was a table, a tape recorder, and four chairs. In one of the chairs was an angry Tom Morrisson.

"You can't keep me here!" he shouted when they first walked in. "I didn't do anything."

Collins stopped in the doorway and turned to Harry. "They all say that," he told him with a smile. "They learned it from *Dragnet*." The black detective looked back at Morrisson while still standing in the doorway, the reports under his arm. "Well, you're absolutely right, Mister Morrisson," Collins answered cheerily. "So we're just going to have a little chat before we can decide what to do with you."

"I want my lawyer," Tom said.

"That's the second line they learn," Collins cracked to Harry, then fully entered the room. "Do you have a lawyer?" the black man asked.

Morrisson thought a little bit. "Not by name," he said.

Callahan was going to warn Collins about the kid's lack of eating and sharp temper when he remembered he hadn't mentioned overhearing their office conversation. But since he was leaning toward the other detective as if to mention something, he spoke up anyway. "He doesn't have one."

"Hmmph," Collins said as he put down the reports and sat in the chair opposite Morrisson. "Well, of course if you don't have a lawyer, the court will assign you one, but first we have to get to court. You understand?"

"I have a lawyer, I have a lawyer!" Tom yelled.

"Give us his name or number so we can call him," Collins suggested.

"Uh . . . uh," Morrisson answered. "Uh . . . give me a phone book. I'll look it up."

"Sorry," said Collins, knowing it to be a ploy by which Tom would call up the most appetizing lawyer he could find, then promise him any amount of money to take on his case. It was a time-wasting routine. "No phone books. They were all ripped off."

Morrisson fell silent. "I guess we'll just have to have a talk without a lawyer," Collins went on. "Now you know all your rights, don't you, Thomas?"

"Tell them to me again."

"Oh you know them," Collins countered affably. "I bet you watch *Barney Miller* every night. Let's get down to cases, shall we?" The black detective looked over at Harry, who was standing off to the side behind him. "You know who Inspector Callahan is, don't you?" Collins inquired.

Harry realized his whole subterfuge could blow up in his face with one wrong word out of Morrisson's mouth. He looked at the kid with no expression, not wanting to tip his hand. If Tom knew that Harry didn't want him to say anything about Shanna, he had no doubt she'd be the primary topic of conversation.

"Yeah," Morrisson snarled. "He's a fucking cop." For one of the few times in his career, Harry didn't mind being called that. To him, it was better than being called "Shanna's uncle."

"Yes," Collins agreed with the kid. "He's a fucking cop who has brought you in on charges of assault with a deadly weapon, resisting arrest, and disturbing the peace. Do you have anything to say to these charges?"

"Do I have anything to say?" Morrisson responded

incredulously. "Do I have anything to say? You bet I have something to say!"

"Remember," Collins said quickly. "Anything you say can be used against you."

Morrisson fell silent again.

"Oh good," Collins said. "Now we can get on with the really neat stuff. First, let's see if we have the right Tom Morrisson. You are Tom Morrisson of 365 Commonwealth Avenue, apartment 4D?"

"Yeah," Morrisson answered miserably.

"The Tom Morrisson who is an undergraduate theater major at Emerson College?"

"Yeah, that's me," Morrisson nodded.

"The Tom Morrisson who is a chairman of the organization called The Order of the Orenda?"

The young man had leaped out of his seat. "How do you know about that?" he shouted, coming around the table. Collins sat unaffected as Harry met Morrisson halfway. Tom looked up into Harry's lined face and thought better of moving anymore. He slowly returned to his seat while Collins laughed.

"Oh, we know a lot about all sorts of different cults that pop up in Boston, Thomas. We make it a practise to find out all we can about all these perverted sects."

Callahan had to admit to himself that Collins knew what he was doing. He had pegged Morrisson as a hopped-up hothead as soon as he entered the room, then degraded Tom's most cherished beliefs in the most callous way he knew. All his words were designed to get a rise out of the kid.

It worked quickly. "It is not a cult!" Morrisson shouted, standing next to his seat. "And it is not perverted! It's the original belief! The belief of the true Americans."

"Yes, we know," Collins responded knowledgeably. "The American Indian beliefs. But there are so many different tribes with so many different beliefs."

"We take the best of all of them," Morrisson cried with pride.

"What?" Collins queried. "Like the Iroquois who believed there was more than one soul which traveled to different places depending on how the body died? Like the Algonquians who believed evil spirits must be driven out of the body for a happier life? Like the Plains Indians, who cut off joints of fingers as a sacrifice?

"Or do you go further?" Collins leaned in, his voice rising in pitch and speed. "Are you like the Pawnee, who murdered young squaws in the name of the morning star? Or are you like the Inca and Maya who didn't need an excuse to raid a neighboring tribe for a virgin sacrifice? Or the Aztec who made special raids to acquire their victims and slaughtered them by the hundreds?"

"No!" Morrisson screamed, clawing across the table for Collins' throat. He gripped the black man's neck just as Callahan swiped him across the room with the back of his hand.

Morrisson flew bodily off the table, traveled three feet through the air, and slid in a crumbled mass against the wall. Collins merely straightened his coat and tie.

"No," Morrisson said feebly from the floor, tears rolling down his cheeks. "I am a shaman. We believe in purity and the Great Spirit. We believe in Brotherhood. . . ."

The boy's words reduced to incoherent babble. Collins rose, looking at the huddled mass in the corner.

"That's about all we can do here," Collins grimaced.

"It's enough," said Harry.

"Yeah," Collins agreed, calling in the uniformed men to take the boy away. "Feel like a little ride?" the black detective asked Callahan when they got out into the hall.

"Sure," said Harry, knowing an order when he heard one. "Why not?" Harry may have outranked Collins, but Boston was the black man's town. He'd have an easier time making things stick than Callahan.

They went downstairs, out the back, and into Collins' unmarked El Dorado. "What's going to happen to the

61

kid?" Harry asked, settling into the plush red passenger seat.

"Probably going to have to send him to the hospital now," Collins mused. "Find out what's making him crazy. Hold him a couple of days for observation."

For the second time, Harry wanted to mention the kid's lack of food, but he had purposely omitted the information before, so he stuck with his little white lie. "What then?" he asked.

"Then," Collins retorted, starting the car's engine, "then we'll probably release him."

Harry sat up. "What?"

"We have a little problem with your charges, Inspector," Collins said pulling out into the sparse night traffic.

"Such as?" Harry inquired, ignoring the many sights along the wide avenues.

"First and foremost," Collins said, watching the road, "the assault with a deadly weapon."

"He attacked a girl with a hunting knife!" Harry said incredulously, his hackles rising. "You mean they don't have a law against that here?"

Rather than responding to Callahan's obvious sarcasm, Collins went curtly to the heart of the matter. "Where's the girl? Where's the knife?"

That caught Harry unawares. Finding Christine should be no problem, but he had assumed that Tom had the knife on him when he ran. "Find the girl and you'll probably find the knife," was what Harry concluded aloud.

"Probably, probably," Collins echoed, turning right onto a wide, two-way street. Harry saw the Boston Gardens, the companion park to the Common to the left at the end of the block. "But until then, we have another deadly weapon to worry about."

Harry didn't like the sound of that. Collins didn't wait for a response. "I mean, after all, it's only your word that Morrisson attacked the girl with a knife. I mean, he didn't attack you with the knife, now did he?" Collins still didn't pause for an answer. "No, from what I hear, he nearly attacked you with a gun until you took it away from him. A big gun. A cannon, Morrisson called it."

Collins looked out the corner of his eye at Callahan again as they stopped for a red light. Harry just stared at the detective. "That's what took me so long," Collins explained. "I had a couple of brothers in the hospital talking real loud about a big white dude who beat up on them with a cannon and, of all things, a ghetto blaster. They wanted to press charges until I talked them out of it. You wouldn't happen to know anything about that deadly weapon, would you?"

Harry picked up the cue. Collins did him a favor by not pushing through the music man's charge of assault, so now Harry was supposed to make it easy on him. Thankfully, it was not just the politest thing to do, it was the wisest. Harry reached into his brown tweed coat and pulled out his Magnum .44. He opened the cylinder, dropped the rounds into his hand, and passed it over to Collins.

"Whooee," the detective whistled softly. "They were right. That *is* a cannon. What is that, a .44 with a . . . how long barrel?"

"Six and a half inch barrel," Harry said tiredly.

"A dude your size I would've pegged as hauling a nickel-plated eight and three-eights incher for sure."

"What it makes up in velocity and sight radius it loses in portability," Harry said flatly.

Collins didn't want to leave it at that, however. He seemed intent on picturing Harry as the laconic, conservative, right-wing cowboy from the West. "Hey, this is the same sort of gun Son of Sam used, isn't it?"

"A misconception. The .44 is a widely used caliber. Berkowitz used a Charter Arms .44. The gun you're holding is a Smith and Wesson Model 29. A Charter Arms gun was also used to shoot George Wallace. A Charter Arms .38 killed John Lennon."

"That company gets around, doesn't it?"

"Makes a lot of police weapons as well," Harry commented.

Collins slipped in the next question casually but quickly. "You got a license to carry this thing in Massachusetts?"

Harry's silence was the best answer. Collins clucked in sympathy. "I wouldn't worry about it, Inspector. I'll put an application through for you as soon as I get to my office. You can pick up your gun when it comes in or when you're about to leave the state, whichever comes first."

"How long does the license take?"

"Oh, about five or six weeks," Collins said as the light went green and he moved the car forward. "A month if I push it."

"Don't bother," Harry said, adjusting to the idea. If he really needed a gun, he had no doubt he could get one where all the criminals did—underground. That song and dance over with, Harry got back to the main topic on his mind. "You seem to know a hell of a lot about Indians," he said by way of introducing the subject.

Collins wanted to fence words some more. "You know a lot about guns."

Callahan didn't want to play. "What was all that about the Order of the Orenda?"

"It's the name of their quasi-religious group," Collins said, tooling up to the Common. "Orenda is the Iroquois name of the spirit that lives inside everything. Did you see that horror movie called *The Manitou?*" Harry shook his head. "It was based on the Algonquian word for the same spirit. Naturally the filmmakers added a lot more blood and guts."

"Naturally," Harry said sourly. "But what do these kids see in something like that?"

"They figure it does Unitarianism one better by going back to the source of true American beliefs. Since the Indians were here first and so noble and put upon, they think their religion was more pure.

"Unfortunately, these kids aren't Indians. They're middle-class Irish, Italian, and English. They tend to get a little carried away."

"What do you mean?" Callahan pressed on.

"Ah, the whole thing about the purity of death and the blood brother shit and the Happy Hunting Ground concepts. It has a tenuous but bothersome connection to the Halliwell girl."

"Who?" Harry asked as they passed the Boston Playboy Club on their right and went up to Tremont Street. "Oh yeah, I forgot I didn't tell you," Collins answered. "Judy Halliwell. She was the girl who was murdered on the Beacon Hill rooftop last night. I thought you said you knew."

"No," Harry corrected as they took a left to pass the Savoy Theater. "I just read in the papers that the victim was an avid volunteer at the Unitarian Church offices. When I saw Morrisson and the girl Christine come out of there today, I made the connection. By the way, what did Morrisson say about the attack? Did he have a reason?"

"He denied the whole thing. Refused to make a statement. Said there was no girl."

"OK, what about the Halliwell girl, then? Where does she come in?"

"Well," said Collins, pulling in front of the Unitarian offices and stopping the car. "The murderer killed her, one of her cats, and another boy named John Monahan. As near as we can tell, Monahan was a mistake. He told his roommates at the dorm where he lived that he was going to a movie at the Charles Street Theater complex. That would put him in the general area of the crime. We're almost sure he just passed by, heard something, and went to investigate. It was another horror number, by the way."

"What was?"

"The movie. A horror movie called *Just Before Dawn*."

Harry had heard of it. He didn't care. He stayed away from that kind of garbage. "We've got enough horror of our own," Callahan reminded the detective. "In reality. How does the Halliwell girl fit in?"

"It's that virgin sacrifice thing," Collins finally admitted. "I mean, the cat getting croaked; that could signify the soul of an animal released. And the rooftop; it could fill in as the sacrificial altar. Finally, there was a piece of information we didn't release to the papers. The Halliwell girl was raped."

"Evidence of semen?" Harry asked.

"No," Collins shook his head. "The killer must've been spooked by Monahan's arrival. According to the coroner, her hymen was broken, then the guy pulled out."

"So she was a virgin."

"Until last night, yeah. And she probably stayed that way until after she died."

Harry swore aloud. Several times. Collins nodded in commiseration. They were not only dealing with a murderer but with a necrophiliac.

"All I can say, Inspector, is that you picked a hell of a time to go vacationing in Beantown," Collins exclaimed. Their business was finished for the moment, so Harry took Collins' stopping in front of the Beacon Street HQ as a cue for his exit. Harry pulled back the latch and opened the door.

"You'll stay in touch?" Collins asked as Harry got halfway out the door.

"I'll call when I get a room," Harry replied, lifting himself out onto the sidewalk.

"I figure it doesn't have to be said," Collins called out the open passenger door, "but call me if you plan to leave town anytime soon."

"You're right," said Harry. "It didn't have to be said." He closed the door. Collins honked once and drove away Harry's Magnum still on his dashboard.

Harry went up the Unitarian office building's steps

The front door was locked. He walked all the way around the building. There were no lights on and no sign of a live-in custodian. Harry walked down the street to the intersection of Beacon and Charles streets. Charles looked far more lively, so he took a right onto it. He walked until he found a drugstore with an old-fashioned wooden telephone booth, complete with a recent directory.

He looked up "Donovan, Shanna." He got the number, slipped a dime in the slot, and dialed. There was no answer after ten rings. He asked the woman behind the counter for directions and walked to Shanna's apartment. It was a cellar room on a side street near the Charles River and Storrow Drive. Harry walked down the steps and knocked.

He waited for fifteen minutes, alternately knocking and sitting. While he waited, he thought. And while he thought, the depression came at him again.

There may have been something in what Linda had said. It didn't seem likely, but Harry had seen stranger things happen in his career. In a world where people killed each other because they didn't like Mondays, anything was possible. It was even possible that out of the millions of families on the Earth, a bunch of starving, knife-wielding Indian lovers had marked Shanna out for an execution.

It had been a rotten day. Superman had taunted him while he was getting an acute case of jet lag, he had broken two radios, he had nearly gotten creamed in an orange Pinto, he had argued with hs favorite kin, and he had broken up a seemingly non-existent attempted murder. Harry was hungry, Harry was tired, and Harry was depressed.

He took the edge off of the first problem by finding a little steakhouse on the corner of Charles and Beacon streets which char-broiled a T-bone to his order. He took care of the latter two problems by taking a piece of paper out of his pocket and searching out the Sack 57 Hotel. It was across the street from a Benihana restaurant and built on top of a Howard Johnson's. He rode up to the eleventh floor empty-handed. He knocked on the door of room 1115. Terri the stewardess, unlike the rest of the women in his life, was in.

She was wearing a beautiful silk robe and that was all. She had let down her golden blonde hair. Without her shoes she came up to Harry's neck. He went to bed with her hoping he'd think he was back in California by the time the sun rose.

She had left when the phone rang the next morning. At first Harry had thought "fuck it," but then he considered that Terri might have had an accident on the way to work. Maybe she hadn't made the plane. Maybe it was her superiors calling to find out if everything was all right. Maybe it was Collins who had found her eye in her handbag and was calling whoever might be there to say that she had been sacrificed to the American Indians' gods. At this point, Harry wasn't disregarding any possibilities. He rolled over and picked up the phone receiver.

"Hello," he said.

"Harry?" was the breathy reply. "Is this Harry, Shanna's relative?"

Harry wanted to think about it, but dealing with a question like that in someone else's hotel room could take a lot longer than the caller was willing to wait.

"Yes," he answered quickly. "Christine?"

"Yes," it was her turn to answer.

"How did you get this number?" was his immediate question.

"Tom gave it to me," was her immediate answer.

"Tom?" Harry said in surprise. He felt a breeze at the back of his neck. Or it could have been a chill, he wasn't sure. "Christine, where are you?"

"I'm at school."

"Emerson?"

"Yes, at the building down the street where Shanna's

apartment is. Harry, you must come right away. I have to talk to you."

"Is Tom there with you now?" Harry asked hastily.

Christine sounded surprised. "No. Of course not."

"When did you last see him?"

"Last night. After you chased him away. He only called me later to apologize for overreacting. He said that you told him to give me this number in case I wanted to get in touch with you."

"All right," said Harry quickly, already sitting up and pulling on his pants. "Stay there. If you're in a class, stay with the group. If you're alone, go outside. Wait for me outside where some other people can see you. If you see Tom, be careful. Find some other people and stay with them. Don't let him get you alone and watch out for any sudden moves."

"Talk about overreacting!" Christine laughed in astonishment. "Tom just went away for a while because he hadn't eaten in a couple of days. Now he's back. It's all right, Harry."

Harry pulled on his shirt. "I'm sure it is, Christine," he soothed. "Just do me a favor. No big deal. Keep your eyes open."

"Sure, Harry," agreed the girl. "Hurry up, will you? All this talk of sudden moves is giving me the creeps."

"I'll be right there. And Christine . . . ?"

"Yes?"

"What's your last name?"

"Sherman," she said without question or hesitation.

They both said good-bye and hung up. Harry slipped on his shoes, pulled on his jacket, went to the hotel-room door, turned completely around, and went back to the phone. He called up the Boston Police. When a sergeant answered, he identified himself and asked for Collins.

"I'm sorry, Inspector, but he left a couple of hours ago to get some sleep," the officer responded.

"I brought a man in last night. Tom Morrisson. Do you know what happened to him?"

"Hold on," said the sergeant, then put Harry on hold. And with no music, either. Harry waited three minutes, then he hung up and left the room.

A taxi was no problem. A few were lining up in front of the hotel. The way his sense of *déjà vu* was going Harry promised himself not to be surprised if his driver was the same one who had tried to bilk the foreigners at the airport. Thankfully for his sense of equilibrium, it wasn't. The ride was mercifully quick; just having to shoot down Charles, take a left at Mount Vernon, then another left. The cabbie dropped Harry off at number 96 without a single traffic light getting in the way. Callahan gave him a handsome tip. Think of it, he mused, an honest taxi driver. The cab drove off, and Harry was alone.

He didn't like it. He was on another narrow Back Bay street at the base of Beacon Hill. He was facing a four-storied rectangular building with thick opaque windows only on the second and fourth floors. There were two doors in the front. Across the street was a brick wall. He looked to the right. A block down was Shanna's building. He looked to the left. A block down was Beacon Street. He could see a section of the Gardens across it.

Christine was not outside. In fact, the area seemed deserted. No, he didn't like it at all. But like it or not, he still approached the left-hand door. He gave it a tug. It opened. He slipped inside, desperately wishing that he still had his Magnum.

The thin, hallway-like foyer was slightly calming. It had all the accoutrements of a college facility. There were flyers about upcoming dances, concerts, and other social events taped to the window of the inside door. To the left was a bigger bulletin board with more information; school plays, blood banks, report due announcements, and the like. To the right was a glassed-in display case full of footballs, pictures, papers, and trophies.

Although it certainly was a school building or a brilliant facsimile thereof, it lacked the one vital ingredient that would make the establishment work. Namely, students and/or teachers.

There was a hallway to Harry's right, lined with junk-food machines on one side and lavatory doors on the other. One was marked "Men," another "Women," and a third was marked "Faculty" whom, as every student knows, fit in neither of the previous two categories.

There was a stairway to Harry's left and on the first platform, some swinging doors to a classroom. Harry stepped up and looked through the glass section of the doors. The large, wood, high-ceilinged room was empty of everything save dozens of desk-winged chairs. About thirty were spread out in front of a blackboard, but the rest were piled up near the windows.

Harry looked up the rest of the stairs. He saw little and heard nothing but his own breathing. He thought about calling for Christine but choked back the name. He had been a cop too long. If, for any reason at all, someone was waiting to do him harm, his yell would tip them off. And if no one was waiting and it was just his paranoia raging, then there was no harm in not calling. In other words, only shouting could cause woe. Not shouting would harm no one.

Harry silently walked up the rest of the stairs. They emptied out onto a dance studio. The big, multimirrored room covered the entire floor. There was no place to hide and, sadly, no Christine present either. Harry wouldn't have minded finding the girl decked out in a leotard practicing. But the only thing he saw was a circular metal stairway across the room, rising to the fourth floor.

He saw light from the final story's windows splashing on the top rungs of the steps. He moved until he could place both hands on the banister. He stopped and listened for several minutes; there was absolutely no sound of human activity up there. Callahan spent several more seconds considering his situation. Could he have the wrong building? No, it was the only college building down the street from Shanna's apartment. Could Christine have taken off of her own free will? Why not? Harry didn't know her at all. She could've gotten bored waiting or had another class.

Callahan caught himself. He was doing the same thing he thought Linda was doing. Taking a possibly minor situation and blowing it up into a major affair. That sort of thing must run in the family, he thought with a stab of mental pain. Then he remembered what Christine had said. Tom had called her. There was absolutely no way Tom could have contacted her unless he had used his one phone-call right to talk to her. But that still didn't explain how Tom or she had known where he was.

The paranoia returned. Something messy was going on, and Harry was in the middle of it. He moved up the spiral staircase smoothly and quickly.

Another studio stretched out in front of him. But this looked to be for an acting class, illuminated by the magnified light coming through the thick, square windowpanes. There were risers and props and curtains hanging everywhere on the ceiling. It looked like a class where at least four scenes were going on at once for four different teachers in four curtained-off sections of the room.

Of all the sights Harry had seen that morning, he liked this the least. There were four places someone could be hiding. He looked around the room. Lying under one of the windows was a metal-tipped wood pole, the kind teachers use to pull down shades that are too high to reach.

It was just what the doctor ordered. Not only would it make his long arm of the law longer, it would serve well as a weapon. It didn't have the range or power of a Magnum but it would have to do. Harry pushed aside the first set of curtains with it. There was nothing there. He moved on to the second.

Christine Sherman was lying face down on the floor behind them.

As soon as he saw her form, he heard the screeching

yell behind him. He tried to turn, but it was too late. A thundering pressure slammed against the back of his head. He felt the pole leave his grip and heard it clatter to the ground beside him. He landed on his face.

The bastard had come in behind him. He had been waiting for Harry and had snuck into the building after him, knowing that it was empty for the day.

Even though the pain blossomed from his skull to his brain like a rapidly growing weed, Callahan tried to hold on, if for no one else's sake but Christine's. He couldn't leave her alone with Morrisson. In his state, there was no telling what the kid might do.

With incredible effort, Harry pushed out with his right arm. At the same time he tried to clear his vision of the bulbous red and orange globes with the thick black streaks. He managed to roll over and clear his vision just as a deeper, darker black fell on top of him.

He had cut the curtains. The bastard had chopped the black curtains down on top of him. Harry couldn't see anything and he couldn't crawl out. He tried, but the cloth acted like a net, and the bastard started hitting him again.

In the recesses of his pain-riddled mind, Harry recognized the sounds of the sweeping arcs of air. The bastard was beating him with the window-shade pole. Distantly, he heard the sound of the thick wood wacking into him. Seemingly seconds after each blow had fallen, he felt the pain. He managed to crawl a few inches on his hands and knees. Then the pole cracked into the top of his head. He stopped, his head bouncing. Again the club came down. It drove him back to the floor this time.

Stupid, was the last thing Harry said to himself before he lost consciousness. You should have played possum. You could have saved yourself a concussion that way.

Callahan woke up. His head felt like a peanut in the trunk of an elephant. He still couldn't see. He raised his hand to lift the black material off him. He wasn't ready for a shroud yet. He kept pushing and pulling until he saw the school's ceiling above him. It was in terrible shape. It looked about as bad as he felt.

He remembered Christine's form on the floor. He looked over to where she had lain. She was no longer there. He gingerly got up to his knees. Although pain centers were playing. "Tubular Bells" in his brain, he managed to go from there to his feet.

He looked all the way around the room. Christine wasn't there. Tom Morrisson was.

He lay face up in a spotlight of blood. Judging by the many slits in his torso, Callahan assumed the blood was Tom's own.

It hurt Harry's head to consider the ramifications of this new situation. He left the corpse there and went downstairs to find a phone.

Chapter Five

"I feel compelled to say, Inspector Callahan, that you are the closest thing to a living Frankenstein's monster I have come across in my thirty years of medical service."

The squat, wispy-haired doctor marveled at the big, rugged man in the hospital bed.

"As chief of staff of this hospital," the doctor went on, "I was brought in on this case. You should feel honored, Inspector. You are very important to the city of Boston."

"I'll try to live up to that," Harry promised sardonically. But the addled, almost senile hospital head was not through yet.

"Incredible," he muttered. "Absolutely incredible. I've never seen so much scar tissue on one human being. Living human being, that is. There are signs of recent serious wounds to your thigh, your shoulder, and your hands. And you suffered many other wounds before that. Incredible. Truly incredible. How do you walk?"

"I manage," Harry answered. "How's my head?"

"Oh yes, your most recent wound," the doctor commented. "Well, you'll continue walking. It is an incredibly strong cranial bone. Some slight contusions here and there but no concussion, and no fracture, thank God. That was what worried me the most. With a fracture you might have seen stars, suffered paralysis, seen things. With a concussion, you might have suffered blackouts occasionally. With a fracture, I doubt if there would be any question about it. Frequent blackouts. Oh yes, quite definitely."

"But I have neither," Harry said.

"Neither what?" said the doctor.

"Concussion or fracture," said Harry.

"Of course not!" said the doctor. "What are you worrying about? I would have told you if you had those."

The nurse poked her head in the room, saving Callahan from any more Boston medical torture. "You have guests, Mr. Callahan."

"Very good," the doctor said as if the nurse had been speaking to him. "I'll be off then. Take care of yourself, Inspector." The little man got up, walked over, but stopped by the door. "Oh, and Inspector?" Harry looked at him. "If, by any chance, things get worse for you, don't bother donating your organs to science. In their condition, they wouldn't do us any good!"

Callahan laughed out loud as the little medico's head disappared after the rest of his body. The hospital head wasn't as pixilated as he seemed. As he left, Mr. and Mrs. Peter Donovan came in.

Linda looked the same, albeit even more worried. It was Peter who had done all the changing for the family. Harry remembered the happy, sandy-haired, square-jawed Mick he had met at his cousin's wedding. The man who came in with that girl now was a different man. The square jaw had sagged along with his belly. The sandy hair had risen across his skull and turned almost white. He kept it in a crew cut.

And the face was anything but happy. It was the face of a man beaten by life. Harry had had his share of bouts with reality as well, but his face showed that he had fought back. Peter looked like he had stood and taken it, fists by his side. He was still a proud Irishman, his biceps thick and his forearms strong, but he also seemed a stubborn, ignorant one.

"Harry, are you all right?" Linda asked, rushing to the chair the doctor had vacated.

"I'm fine, Linda. Just had a little accident." He was still sitting up in bed, having accommodated the doctor's checkup. The ugly bruises on his chest could be seen by all. Linda's mouth shaped itself into a silent "Oh," when she saw the black-and-blue welts. She touched one with her finger. Harry didn't like the expression on Peter's face when she did. It was one of barely controlled jealousy. A look of possession and anger at the same time.

It disappeared when Peter joined his wife by the side of the bed. His body language spoke for him then. He placed both hands on her shoulders, practically pulling her to his side.

"We were worried about you," he said without much conviction.

Harry began to put himself in Peter's place. His business was failing. His daughter was getting out of hand. His wife was getting desperate. And all along he had considered himself the champion of the world; the one guy who was going to make it. And now his wife had even called for a distant cousin over him. He must've felt like living shit.

"Fine. No problem," said Harry.

"Did you see Shanna?" Linda asked. Harry saw Peter's hands tighten on her shoulders. He thought he saw the man grimace slightly. Linda looked up at him for a split second, then looked back at Harry imploringly.

"Yes," he told her. "We talked."

"You see?" said Peter. "I told you she'd talk to her old 'Uncle Harry.' You see, there's no problem, really." The man was forcing his casualness just a bit stridently. "I told her, Harry, I really did. I said, 'This is just your imagination, Lin.' You know what I mean, don't you, Harry? A daughter goes out on her own for the first time, and the mother starts imagining all sorts of crazy things."

Harry smiled without humor. Tom Morrisson's corpse was not part of his imagination.

"She called," Linda told him. "Last night . . . after you left her. She called to say that she was all right."

"It was a good talk," Peter interjected over his wife's words. "You really did the trick, Harry. You made her think about how concerned we were about her. So everybody really communicated."

Harry concentrated on Peter again. He had a smile on his face, but the rest of his expression was strained. Those weren't his words he was saying. He was as uncomfortable expressing them as Harry was hearing them.

"She says she's really 'getting her act together,' " the father went on. "She says her boyfriend really helps. She says she really feels necessary for the first time in her life."

Linda looked up between her husband's gripping hands. "She didn't say that to me."

Peter tightened his grip, speaking to Linda while looking apologetically at Harry. "I guess you were off the phone then, dear."

Linda wouldn't leave it at that. "She won't let us meet her boyfriend," she told Harry conspiratorially.

"Now, Linda . . .," Peter mocked, looking up at the ceiling.

"Well, she won't, Peter!" she said to him. She leaned over toward Harry. "We've never seen him. She won't bring him over. He won't call while she is with us. I don't like it, Harry. I don't like it at all."

Harry didn't like it either. Not that Shanna's boyfriend was a stranger, but that he was brought up at this point at all. The play Harry felt he was in kept having its author changed. First it was Harold Pinter, then it was Samuel Beckett, now it was Edward Albee and "Who's Afraid of Harry Callahan?"

"She just hasn't had the chance yet, honey," Peter patiently explained. "You know how kids are, Harry. They get so wrapped up in schoolwork and everything."

"And everything," Harry seemed to agree. "Well, at least you know the boy's name, right?"

"We practically had to drag it out of her . . . !" Linda began.

"Jeff Browne," Peter interceded. "A real nice guy."

"How would you know?" Linda spat. "We've never met him."

Peter looked patiently down. "Because Shanna told me, that's why. And I, for one, believe what my own daughter says."

It was a verbal slap that hit its mark. Linda looked at her husband, then at Harry. She bit her lower lip, her eyes misted, and she quickly looked at the floor.

"I'm glad you're all right, Harry," she said in a small voice. "Thanks for all your help." She couldn't go on. She pulled out from under her husband's grip and ran out of the room.

Harry's face was an expressionless mask. Peter watched her go, then stared at the empty doorway for several seconds. When he turned back to the cop, his grin was a sheepish one.

"Jesus, women," he said by way of explanation. Rubbing the back of his crew-cut head, he sat down in the vacated chair to try verbally to figure it out. "Well, she's so wrapped up and all. This whole thing has gotten her worked up."

"What whole thing?" Harry asked quietly.

"Well, that Beacon Hill murder and all," Peter answered. "You know, because Shanna knew the dead girl. But she says it's OK. I mean, a lot of people get murdered, and all their friends don't fall apart, do they?"

"Yeah," Harry agreed slowly. "A lot of people get murdered."

"Well, everything's getting better now," Donovan concluded. "We're all getting over it. Just a few more days and everything'll be back to normal." He put a calloused hand reluctantly on Harry's shoulder. "I really want to thank you for all your help. You really did the trick."

It was the big kiss-off, Harry realized. Both Linda and Peter were trying to tell him good-bye, bon voyage, be sure to write. They didn't know about the Morrisson murder yet. No one knew except Harry, the police, and the murderer. Unless. . . .

Harry was suddenly very sorry he came. He really didn't need to know that Shanna was involved with an Indian cult. He really didn't want to suspect that Shanna was involved with murder. He could have very happily stayed in San Francisco, up to his neck in other people's blood.

He returned Peter's smile. His was as lifeless and as fake as Donovan's. "That's all right," he murmured. "Least I could do."

"We have your luggage here," Peter spoke up quickly. "It's out in the hall. You want me to put it in the closet here?" He motioned at the little cupboard in the private room.

"Sure," Harry agreed. It wasn't merely a kiss-off, Harry thought. It was a kick-out. They were rolling up the red carpet while he was still on it.

Peter brought the two cases in. While he was hanging up the suit bag, he started talking anew. "Uh, listen, Harry. I really appreciate all you've done. I really do. But given the circumstances, maybe it would be better if you dropped the whole thing. You know what I mean?"

Harry had no intention of making it easy for the man. "No, not really. What circumstances do you mean?"

"Well, the murder and all," Peter said, still busying himself in the closet. "You know, everybody's all excited and worried and nervous. And you being a detective and all, well. . ." Peter's hands fluttered around his waist like falling leaves. "It just sort of stirs up a lot of mud that would stay at the bottom of the river otherwise. You know what I mean?"

Peter was trying to say "lay off" in his most subtle manner. Harry suddenly wanted the conversation over with very quickly. Then he sincerely hoped that afterward he would never set eyes on Linda's husband again. "I'm beginning to get the picture," he said.

"Good," Peter said, turning toward him with relief. "That's great. I mean, you understand, right? It just would be for the best if you would just sort of, well, you know. . . ." His hands continued their incomprehensible sign language near his belly.

"Yeah," said Harry. "I know."

Peter nodded, then looked around the room for something else to say. "Take care of yourself, Harry," was what he finally came up with. Then he, too, was gone.

Callahan stared at an empty stretch of wall for a couple of seconds. Then he threw back the bedcovers and started to get dressed. He had pulled on his pants when Detective Christopher Collins came sweeping into the room, a package under his arm.

"Leaving so soon?" the black cop drawled. "And I just ordered flowers, too."

Harry slipped on his shoes, giving Collins a tired look. "I don't like the smell," he said.

"You should wash more," Collins commented, sitting in the one seat next to the bed. "Warm," he commented about the seat. "Had visitors?"

"I love a parade," Harry replied. He was going to say more when he realized that Collins ostensively didn't know about Callahan's relatives. "What brings you here?" he asked, aware of the absurdity of the question.

Collins responded in kind. "We're still having some problem with your charges. Your assaulter with a deadly weapon is dead, and there's still no deadly weapon."

Harry glanced up. "But you picked up Christine Sherman?"

"No Christine Sherman either."

Harry sat down heavily on the edge of the bed, his shirt still off. "What happened?" he asked, amazed.

"What do you mean?" Collins responded, still acting difficult. "How did Morrisson get out, how did Sherman get away, or how did the murder take place?"

"Start from the beginning," Callahan spat, getting up to find another shirt in his bag.

"Morrisson went crazy in the car taking him to the hospital. He jumped out along Storrow Drive and disappeared into Beacon Hill. We called most of the hotels in the city to find you. You weren't available. Where the hell did you sleep last night?"

"With a friend," Harry said simply. "You would've needed her name to locate me."

"Bad show," Collins critiqued. "The Boy Scout motto is 'Be Prepared.' The cop's motto is 'Be Available.' "

"I'm out of uniform, too," Harry scowled, buttoning the light green shirt. "Want to sue me?"

"All right, all right. Anyway that's the last we heard about Morrisson until your call."

"You look up Sherman's address?"

"Yeah, she wasn't at home. An APB is out on her. No response yet."

"What the hell happened?" Harry repeated, more for his own benefit than anyone else's.

"You want to know the official Boston PD version of the events?" Collins inquired sweetly. Harry nodded, leaning on the baseboard of the bed. "Morrisson gets away, his hopped-up head giving him visions of another virgin sacrifice. He gets to the Sherman girl and drags her up to the highest location immediately available. In this case it is the fourth floor of the Emerson school building. Then he's all set to stick her when you come in. He beats the hell out of you, but that gives Christine time to wake up, grab the knife, and in a frenzy kill him."

"That doesn't explain everything," Harry complained.

"They rarely do," Collins freely admitted. "We just do the best we can with the facts available."

"All right," said Harry. "Question one: why did the girl call me, and how did she get my number?"

"Morrisson could've seen you and followed you," Collins suggested. "You were still in the Unitarian HQ area. He could've been staking out the place for Christine and seen you instead."

"But why call Christine and give her the room number?"

"Maybe he wanted to kill two birds with one stone. It was just that before he could kill you, Christine woke up and got the better of him."

"And what happened to her then?"

"Well, picture it, Inspector!" Collins theorized. "A good friend, a good-looking boy you thought you knew, goes crazy with a knife, kidnaps you, and tries to kill you. Terrified, you strike back. Now horrified, you realize you've murdered a person in cold blood. You're confused, you're frightened. So you run."

Harry couldn't fight the re-creation. It didn't sit right with him, but there was nothing he could think of to suggest. "That's it, then?" he inquired.

"As far as my superiors are concerned," Collins revealed, stretching his legs. "They're grooming me for another case. All we're doing is waiting until the Sherman girl is spotted. Then we'll wrap up this whole messy thing. Everybody is just thankful that we kept the body count on this one down to three. Not counting the cat, of course. There was the possibility of a whole string of sacrificial murders."

"No chance now, huh?" Harry grunted, pulling on his tweed jacket.

"Now I didn't say that," Collins wound up slowly. "I'm still worried a little bit. Morrisson wasn't the only shaman of the Order, you know. There was a kid higher than him. The boss of the business, in fact. He could have had something to do with the killings. He could have been the one who planned and implemented the whole thing with Morrisson as his hired dupe."

"So why don't you go after him?"

"I'm not on the case anymore, Inspector," Collins reminded him. "And I can't convince my bosses about the possible dangers."

Harry came around the bed and stood looking down at

the seated black man. "That's tough," he said carefully.

Collins didn't look back at him. Instead he pulled the package out from under his arm. "Oh by the way," he said casually, "that application you made out came through today." He handed the package to Harry.

Inside was the .44 Magnum, complete with a duly authorized and dated license to carry it on his person in Boston.

"I wouldn't go hunting any taxis with it," Collins suggested, "but the city streets are so dangerous nowadays. Tourists need all the protection they can get."

Harry silently retrieved his shoulder holster, replaced the weapon, and slipped the whole rig on under his jacket. He looked at Collins in expectation, hoping the cop wouldn't make him ask for the name of the other Orenda head.

Instead of talking, Collins merely put a scrap of paper down on the side table, rose, neatened his tan coat, and headed for the door. "Take care of yourself, Inspector," he said breezily, as if he were afraid someone might be listening. "Thanks for all your help." He stopped with the door half-open. "And keep in touch," he said meaningfully.

Once he had gone, Harry shook his head in wonder. He almost wished he had been dreaming it all. The Donovans wanted him to leave. Linda was reluctant, but Peter had convinced her of it. But who had convinced Peter? By the sound of it, Shanna had come down on her parents harder than Harry had any right to expect. It could have been done out of embarrassment, but it also could've been done out of fear. Fear that Harry would find out more about the things she was involved in than she wanted him to know.

Whatever the reason, it seemed as if Shanna had told her parents that she didn't want or need Harry's help, and they had come to Callahan with the message. Collins, on the other hand, wanted him to stay. The police hierarchy had handcuffed him, so he wanted Harry to be his unofficial private eye. He wanted Harry to tidy up the edges of the operation, checking things he couldn't.

And the black detective had gone out on a limb to do it. He hadn't pulled strings to get Harry a gun license overnight; he'd gone and pulled a full-fledged rope! That kind of influence impressed Harry. Collins knew what he was about and was willing to risk his neck to make sure justice was served.

No matter what any of them had wanted, Harry had already decided to stay his entire time in Boston. He owed it to Christine, if no one else. If Collins was right and she had killed Morrisson before he could kill Harry, the San Francisco cop had a debt to repay.

The first step in finding the Sherman girl was talking to Shanna. Then, with or without her blessing, he wanted to see this boyfriend of hers, this Jeff Browne. Harry was already pissed at Jeff Browne. He didn't like the way the subject of his existence had come up. Linda had been pulling at straws, trying to find anything to say that would make Harry stay and look into things further. She must have known that the sudden mention of his existence would pique Harry's interest.

Harry collected his stuff and left the room. Just before his exit, he palmed the paper Collins had left for him. After Shanna and Jeff, Callahan pondered, he'd pay a little visit to the cult head. He'd have to see just what kind of person he was, whether he was capable, as Collins suspected, of hatching as perverted a plan as brainwashing another boy to commit murder.

Callahan stopped at the check-out desk. He discovered his bill had been taken care of by the city of Boston. The cashier looked none too happy about it. She realized it would be a long time before the hospital saw their money. It was taking intercity police cooperation and hospitality a bit far, but Harry was still fairly thankful to Collins for it. He guessed the black detective figured that Harry was more apt to follow through if he were happy. And with his medical costs paid and his Magnum back in place, Harry was supposed to owe him something.

It was time to start paying Collins back. Harry walked toward the exit, folding open the scrap of paper Collins had left. When he read the name of the Orenda chief, he started running for the exit. He crumpled the paper and threw it angrily at a standing ashtray as he passed. The address was obliterated on the scrap but the name was still legible. "Jeffrey Browne," it read.

The hospital was on the corner of Charles Street and Storrow Drive, just under the Back Bay Bridge into Cambridge. Harry passed under the bridge, looking up and down the street. He saw the Charles Street Theater complex a couple of blocks down the way, flanking the base of Beacon Hill on its west side. Farther up the road was Government Center. The marvelous thing about Boston, Harry was learning, was that every section was within a twenty-minute walk of every other one. The other nice thing was that in every section of town, there was a decent place to stay.

Harry was in no mood to appreciate matters, however. He saw the Holiday Inn sign right next to the movie marquees and trotted up. He strode into the lobby, hastily registered, threw his bags at a bellboy, tipped him in advance, took his key, and left without seeing the room.

It was a nice day in Boston. The sun was out, and the temperature was tipping the thermometers at sixty-five degrees. Harry didn't appreciate that either. About the only thing he grimly noted was that his hotel was within reasonable distance from Shanna's apartment and from the Unitarian Headquarters on the other side of the Hill.

Harry charged in that direction. He went weaving up one street then to the right along another. He kept cutting over that way until he reached the north base of the Hill in the middle of Charles Street.

The tail had been impossible to miss. Up on Beacon Hill—where the narrow cobblestone streets were nearly always empty—the young man nonchalantly following Harry from one twist to the next turn was ludicrously obvious, no matter how hard he tried to stay inconspicuous.

There were three possibilities, Harry deduced as he crossed Charles, heading toward Shanna's apartment with the tail in tow. The Donovans could have asked a friend to watch Harry so that he wouldn't bother their little girl. That was unlikely. Collins could have convinced his superiors that Harry was the real murderer, and they needed to waste another officer to keep an eye on him. Also doubtful. That left one possibility. The Order of the Orenda was getting nervous.

Harry welcomed their agitation. It would make his job that much easier. He continued unerringly toward Shanna's place. He caught her just as she was going out. Callahan handled the situation carefully. He couldn't just come out and ask her about Browne or accuse her of complicity. She would close down faster than a gin mill on a Sunday night.

"I'm a little late," he said, surprising her. "Is dinner still warm?"

She whirled about at the sound of his voice, dropping her thin leather gloves in the process. But her reaction upon seeing him was not what he had expected. She laughed at his line, effortlessly. She honestly seemed to think it was funny. Then she put her hands on her hips and acted like an irate wife whose husband didn't come home until late.

"Where were you last night? My roast was ruined!"

It was the one response Harry hadn't been prepared for. He was expecting a nervous cover-up or an ashamed diversion. Instead, Shanna was acting as if Harry was her favorite friend. As if she were really happy to see him.

At first, all his concern and doubt left him. He saw her as she seemed to be: innocent, beautiful, and alive. Then his fears returned, doubled. If she was as she seemed to be, then she might still be in terrible danger. If she wasn't, then Harry was subjugating his senses because he had once loved her.

Callahan pulled himself back on track. He leaned over and scooped up her gloves. "Things got a bit hectic," he told her honestly.

She took them from him. "You should have called," she reprimanded. "I was looking for you everywhere."

"Didn't Christine tell you where I was?" Harry asked in surprise.

"Christine?" Shanna echoed. "No, I didn't see her after she left."

Harry was getting dizzy from all the sudden changes in the situation. Somebody wasn't telling the truth, and the way things were going, there was a distinct possibility that no one was talking straight. If Christine hadn't gone back to the Unitarian offices that night, where did she go and why? And if she had, why didn't Shanna see her, or why didn't she admit having seen her?

Those questions led to even more. And more after that. Harry didn't bother asking himself because he already knew he didn't have the answers. And since no one else seemed inclined to fill in the blanks, Callahan decided it was about time he started finding things out for himself.

He forced himself to stop picturing Shanna as the guileless, delightful child he had been an uncle to. He stopped seeing her now as a beautiful young woman in a lot of trouble. She was a means to an end. Somewhere in her mind was the first step out of this mess. He had to use whatever means necessary to get to it. He felt the Magnum hanging heavily under his arm. His nickname was not

Uncle Harry. It was Dirty Harry. If he didn't want to leave Boston in a box, he had better live up to the name.

"That's funny," Callahan said to the girl cursorily. "She said she was going back to the office." Before Shanna could pursue the matter, Harry changed the subject. "Where are you headed?"

Shanna easily forgot about the Christine question. "I've got a doctor's appointment and then some classes. You want to walk with me?"

Harry thought she'd never ask. They set off down toward Beacon Street. Shanna was wearing the same tight, faded jeans she had had on when Harry first saw her. Only today she had topped them with a black turtle-neck pullover that had shrunk slightly in the wash. Not only did it cling to her closely and set off her flaming hair, but there was a quarter of an inch between the bottom of the sweater and the top of the denims. It was an extremely subtle showing of skin, but extremely effective as well. The little girl Harry had known had grown up into a sensual female.

Shanna seemed unconcerned by her sexual effect as they walked down the street. She seemed unconcerned about most everything, even as they passed the Emerson building Harry had been attacked in. Both doors were chained shut.

"What happened there?" Harry asked innocently.

"Don't know," said Shanna, raising her head to the early afternoon sun for warmth. "When I got up this morning it was already locked."

Collins must've been keeping the Morrisson death secret. If he thought Jeff Browne had anything to do with Halliwell's death, he didn't want to spook him by announcing his dupe's murder.

Shanna took a right onto Beacon Street. Harry followed. The man following Harry also followed.

"You said a doctor's appointment," Harry reminded her, keeping up the banter. "You don't look sick."

"I'm not," Shanna replied earnestly. "He's just my counselor who also happens to have a doctorate."

"Your counselor?"

"Yeah, college counselor. Everybody at Emerson has one. They're members of the staff who get together with you once a week to help you adjust to the 'college experience' as they call it. But basically, it's like a free shrink."

Harry marveled at the progress universities had made. It wasn't like school when he was twenty. Now every kid had their own private nursemaid.

"It's really great," Shanna professed. "He's really helped me get myself together." She could see from Harry's expression as they turned onto Newbury Street that the cop didn't completely buy it. The girl decided to take the bull by the horns.

"It's like he doesn't know you at all," she said quietly. "You are whoever you want to be with him. He doesn't remember your past so he doesn't have any preconceptions of you. You can look at yourself objectively because of that."

Callahan heard and understood. "How long does that take?"

"Dr. Gerrold keeps his schedule loose. Sometimes we talk for a couple of minutes, sometimes the session takes hours. I don't have my first class until three, so we can take our time."

It was what Harry had wanted to know. He needed Shanna out of the way so he could confront Browne without interruption. He left her at the door of the doctor's office. Newbury Street was a Bohemian section of the city. Each side of the street was lined with cafes and art galleries. Gerrold's office was in between a record store and a cheese shop.

She was safe there, Harry thought. At least for a while. He looked back at her from across the street. She had been waiting for him to do that. She was half-in and half-out the doctor's door, looking at Harry's retreating figure. When he turned, she waved and smiled brightly.

Harry waved back, then turned to go after her boyfriend, Jeff Browne.

Chapter Six

While Shanna Donovan was getting her head together, Cathy Bryant was getting murdered. She wasn't an Emerson student. She wasn't a Unitarian. She was a cocktail waitress in Brookline, a quiet suburb of Boston. Her only crime was being too good-looking and parking her car in the same place every day.

She was supposed to check in at about four so she could eat and set up before the restaurant opened at five. The restaurant was just one of several establishments in the little suburban plaza. It nestled amid a ski shop, a bank, and an investment firm, all held together by a large concrete shell.

Underneath these establishments was a two-story underground garage. Cathy had fallen into the habit of parking her Volvo in the third space to the right in front of the elevators.

It was still an hour before the other places closed. It was still an hour before the restaurant opened. It was the quietest time of the business day. Cathy pulled into the usually deserted parking facility and tooled over to her spot. There was a big, dark car in the second space in front of the elevators. Seeing no reason to be concerned, she pulled in. Turning off the engine, she checked her appearance in the rearview mirror.

Long blonde hair. Blue eyes. About five-five. Wearing

a dark suit with slit skirt, high heels, and a tight, silky shirt. A thin band of gold around her neck. Pearl earrings the size of BB shots. While Cathy was checking, so was her killer.

She picked up her bag, which matched the color of her shirt, pulled back the door handle, and slid out. She closed the door. She was grabbed from behind by her breasts and slammed headfirst onto the roof of her car.

The pain in her chest and her head mingled and exploded numbly across her body. She felt herself falling. She felt something reach in under her skirt and between her legs. Something else wrapped around her neck.

Dimly, she saw the door of the other car open in front of her. She felt herself being propelled into the back seat. She fell forward heavily onto the richly padded seat. Her mind started to clear as she felt the clutching, spasmodically clawing fingers on her breasts again. She felt a weight on her back and wheezing breath on the back of her neck. She regained control of her muscles just as she became aware of the knife.

Cathy fought back. She threw up her right arm, feeling it connect with flesh. She heard a sudden, hissing exhalation as the weight atop her yielded somewhat. She twisted her torso, then managed to turn all the way over onto her back.

Her murderer was sitting on her hips in the back seat of the car. She saw the killer's face and the knife in the killer's hand. She couldn't put the two together. It didn't make sense. The shock interrupted her escape attempt, and by the time she tried moving again, it was too late.

The killer was taking no chances. The knife was at the girl's throat, and the slit in her skirt was torn all the way to the waist. Everything beneath was ripped off. Then the ripping hand pressed tightly over Cathy's mouth. The killer leaned in. Cathy began to hyperventilate. She was going into shock. Her eyelids fluttered, and then she fainted.

She never regained consciousness. Through the rear

window of the dark car, a knife could be seen rising and falling, rising and falling.

Harry slammed his fist in the tail's face like a piston. Turning the tables on the man following him had been no problem. From Newbury Street, Harry had walked back to Beacon Hill. He had kept going until he had passed Government Center and was amid the Italian North End, which seemed to have the same design as the rest of Back Bay, only its buildings were more rundown, more closed in. And there was the smell of tomato gravy everywhere—even in the garbage.

Harry's tail had not been a pro. All Callahan had had to do was move ahead a little faster, slip into the mouth of an alley, then wait for the guy to come trotting by. Packing all his frustration behind his right elbow, he had waited until the follower realized his mistake and turned toward him. Then Harry had released all his aggression in a straight-arm shot.

The tail's head snapped back as Harry's other hand wrapped around his shirt front. As the man tried to fall back, Harry jerked him forward into the alley. The street was empty of witnesses, but even if there had been someone there, Callahan doubted if anything would be done. In almost any major Italian section of any major city, this sort of thing had come to be expected.

The young man fell into the alley on his face. But he was resilient. His mind cleared as soon as he hit the ground, and he rolled over onto his back, preparing to leap up. Foreseeing this, Harry had dropped as the man was falling. When he had rolled over onto his back, Harry had put one knee on his chest and the Magnum in his nose.

"I'm looking for Jeff Browne. Could you give me directions?"

If the tail had considered arguing before, the big opening at the end of the .44 barrel changed his mind. He gave Harry Browne's address and agreed to lead the cop there. Harry put the gun away and helped the tail to his feel.

They walked down to the end of the winding North End street and came out on the water's edge. They were in a particularly wealthy section of Boston Harbor, which the city and private industry had been renovating for the past half-decade. "What's your name?" Harry asked as they moved west, back toward the main part of town.

"You're doing a terrible thing, you know," was the tail's answer. "You have no right to persecute the Order of the Orenda. We do only good. We're not a cult. We're not like the Scientologists. We don't stand around on street corners begging."

"No, you just skulk around in alleys, following people."

"Jeff was just worried about Shanna, that's all!" the young man complained. "He didn't like the way things were going. He thought the police were trying to pin those Beacon Hill Murders on us. Just because Judy worked at the Unitarian Church."

"How did you find me?" Harry asked. He figured it was an easier question. The tail could come back to remembering his name when he was ready.

"After Shanna's folks were told you were in the hospital, they told Shanna. Shanna told Jeff."

"And Jeff told you," Harry finished for him. He nodded. It made sense. It may not have been the truth, but it made sense. There was still the question of how Christine had known where to find him before.

"Man, you must be made of steel," the tail commented. "We heard you had the crap beaten out of you, but I had just gotten to the hospital when you came out."

That was him, all right, Harry acknowledged, the man of steel. He might have been faster than a speeding bullet, but it wasn't doing him a hell of a lot of good.

They passed through Boston's Chinatown and into the one-block-long German section of the city. The tail moved down a street to their left. Harry looked down the

96

street to their right. He saw the infamous "Combat Zone." Somehow, the politicians, porn merchants, and the fates had combined to localize the X-rated shops and clubs on a two block radius of the city—sandwiched between the main shopping district and Chinatown.

Every porno store, theater, bar, and whorehouse was located along this one small stretch. It officially ended on one side at the corner Harry was standing on and on the other side at the closed-down Paramount Theater. Harry looked away and followed the tail down the opposite street. They stopped at the entrance to a pedestrian apartment house. It was the least appealing dwelling Harry had run into since his arrival.

"Jeff comes from New York," the tail said, seeing the look on Callahan's face. "He likes this place. It reminds him of home."

"Which apartment is he in?" Harry asked.

"Cellar room," the man replied. "B-2."

"It figures," Harry muttered, pulling open the door and motioning the tail to enter.

The tiny foyer cut off all the Boston sunlight from outside. The space was illuminated by a single naked bulb as was the hallway inside. The entryway was classic, even in so rundown a building. There were a bunch of mailboxes along one wall and a bunch of buttons along the other. Usually there were name tags identifying the apartment dwellers next to the buttons. Not in this building.

Callahan examined the buttons. He could hardly see the identifying numbers etched in a thin metal strip attached to the wall. He looked at the tail. The young man was leaning against the second door, hands in his pockets, looking miserable. "Hey, you," Harry said.

The tail looked up, pointed at himself in surprise, and said, "Me?"

"No, Mahatma Gandhi. Who do you think I'm talking to? Give me something to call you. It doesn't have to be a name, I don't care."

The tail thought about it. "Tim," he decided.

"Tim, get over here," Harry instructed. "Press Jeff's buzzer. Don't fuck around. I'm not here to crucify anybody. I just want to get some answers."

The tail moved his finger around the rows of buttons, then pressed the second one up along the first column. There was no answer. Tim pressed it again. Still no response. Tim looked up at Callahan and shrugged.

Harry pulled a credit card out of his pocket. "We'll wait for him," he said. "Inside." With a simple push and a sudden twist, the locked entry door popped open.

"Why didn't you do that in the first place?" Tim asked, exasperated.

"I wanted to see if Browne was home," Harry answered, pulling the tail in front of him and lightly pushing him toward the stairs.

The interior of the place was worse than the outside. The smells of pulpy wood, kitty litter, and urine combined to create an aroma unsurpassed anywhere else in Boston. The cellar stairs had a pronounced starboard list, and the basement hall looked like a subway tunnel.

The two went over to the door marked 2. Only a pale shadow of the "B" remained. Harry leaned up against one side of the door. Tim took a post on the other side. Callahan checked the area for possible exits. It was an incredible rattrap. Paint was peeling everywhere, and the lighting was so bad, Harry could hardly make out his feet at the ends of his legs.

At the end of the hall was an emergency exit. Harry pointed it out to Tim and put up a finger to mean "just a second." He went over and tried the latch. It wouldn't budge. It was locked. Great, Harry thought. Not only a rattrap, but a fire trap. He returned to Tim, secure in the knowledge that no one was getting in or out that way.

Tim couldn't take the gloom or the silence for long. "I don't get it," he suddenly said. "Why us? Why pick on the Order of the Orenda?"

"Bad luck," said Harry, keeping the death of Morrison

to himself. "Bad timing." The thought of the tall, intense Orenda shaman reminded Callahan of something that had been bothering him. Something Morrisson had said. Perhaps Tim could clear up that mystery. "How do you see the wolf?" Harry asked nonchalantly.

The tail looked over in surprise. "No lip," Harry warned him.

"It's a method of enlightenment," Tim reported. "You fast and meditate until the spirit of the wolf comes to you. The wolf is the Indian's friend. To be visited by the wolf is a white man's greatest honor."

Callahan listened patiently in the dank, decrepit hallway. "Isn't that a little ridiculous?" he asked.

Tim looked the other way. "Fat lot you know," he muttered. "You probably never even got high."

Callahan snorted in amusement. He glimpsed something on the floor. He looked closer. The wood was darker around his shoes than it had been. He knelt down. The floor around his feet was covered with blood.

It was drooling out from under the door of apartment B-2.

Harry pulled out the Magnum and kicked in the door at the same time. The bolt split open and the wood partition swung in, hit something, and moved back. Callahan was already moving forward. He met the door with his shoulder. It swung in again.

A table laden with stuff was smashed to the side. As it was thrown out of the door's path, Callahan took in the rest of the room like a camera's eye. It was a small, dark, cramped, and cluttered room. Everywhere there was Indian paraphernalia. Masks with bulging eyes and thick dark lips covered the walls. A pair of snowshoes hung on a doorknob. Beadwork and stitchings were lying on the floor, on tables, and on almost every other surface. Harry saw animal skins, pottery, carved bowls, arrowheads, a chart of Indian symbols, and a small totem pole in the corner.

In the middle of the room was a dead blonde girl.

Callahan moved forward. He felt a push at his back. He lost his balance just as a tomahawk thudded into the wall behind him. He landed on top of the woman's corpse. He glanced behind him. Tim had his hands out and was hunched over. He had pushed Harry out of the way. He stared in bewilderment at the dead girl, then started to throw up.

Harry looked back to where the tomahawk had come from. He saw a man with a full beard push through a swinging door on the other side of the room. He jumped up and went after him.

"Watch it," Tim managed to choke out. "He's great with those things."

"Those things" turned out to be knives. Harry kicked open the door. It led to the kitchen. He dove in just as a heavy ceremonial blade chunked into the wood of the doorjamb.

There was a window at the end of the dirty kitchen. Cockroaches scurried away as the bearded man threw open the metal grate in front of the glass and Harry dragged his gun up from under him.

The bearded man threw himself right through the pane as he pushed the grate closed behind him. Harry pulled the Magnum's trigger at the same time. The .44's massive boom reverberated through the tile and rattled some dishes. They fell as the bullet tore through one of the grate's metal slats, sending off thick sparks.

Harry pulled himself up as Tim stumbled in. "What the hell is going on?" he screamed in confusion and panic.

Callahan ignored him as he tore open the grate and looked outside. The bearded man was vaulting a fence on the other side of a garbage-strewn yard. Harry pulled off another shot which punched a hole in the wooden fence in between the man's legs.

"Who is that girl?" Tim screeched in the cop's ear.

Harry whirled toward him. "Don't you know her?"

"No!"

Harry leaped out the window. "Call the police. Get them over here."

"But what's going on?" came Tim's frightened, plaintive cry from behind him as he ran for the fence. "What is happening? I don't understand what could have happened!"

Callahan vaulted over the wooden partition in one leap. He landed on his feet in a back alleyway between blocks. He saw the bearded man speeding toward the street. Harry anchored his feet on the asphalt and held his Magnum out in front of his face with two hands. He pointed the barrel right in the middle of the bearded man's back just as the runner was getting to the mouth of the alley. His finger tightened on the trigger.

A car turned the corner into the alley. Both the bearded man and Harry were taken by surprise. The Magnum boomed and bucked in his hand.

The bearded man fell over onto the hood of the car. The bullet sped over his head and tore through the center of the windshield. It smashed out the rear window as the bearded man got up and scrambled across the car's roof.

For one of the few times in his life, Harry felt a cold helplessness. Even in the worst situations, he had always kept faith in his abilities. But now, here, he may have shot an innocent bystander. The chill that coursed through him did not freeze him out of action, however. As he felt the numb rage of a mistake inside him, his legs were already throwing him forward after the bearded man. If he had hurt anyone who didn't deserve it, he wanted to be damn sure he got the one who did.

He saw the bearded man fall off the trunk of the car and scramble around the alley corner at the same time he saw the middle-aged couple in the car blink, look around, and generally act unhurt. Harry paused for a split second in front of the stalled auto.

"Are you all right?" he shouted.

"You fucking maniac!" said the pot-bellied driver. "You could have killed someone!"

Harry had jumped onto the hood even before the man had formed the obscenity. He wouldn't be raging if he or a loved one was hurt. As the man finished his curse, Callahan was in the street twenty feet behind the bearded man.

The bearded man was in the traffic, where there were too many other innocent bystanders. Harry kept the gun out to keep them out of his way and ran into the street. He held his free hand out in a stop signal and kept the .44 up in case he got a clear shot at the bearded man.

The bearded man made it across the street to the accompanying wail of car horns and tire screeches. He disappeared around the corner into the Combat Zone. Harry smiled grimly. It was going to be a hell of a hunt. He poured on the steam and crossed the same distance in three long steps. He was on the sidewalk, at the wall, then around the corner in time to see the bearded man duck into a bookstore three doors down.

Callahan pushed by some shocked pedestrians. He went by two doors, becoming vaguely aware of some non-pornography material in the window of the third building. Harry stopped just before he got to the door. He looked at the items on sale and nearly groaned. It was one of those all-purpose dives that not only sold porno, but jewelry, watches, sunglasses, and weapons as well.

Just as in many of these X-rated sections of other cities, the shops weren't allowed to sell guns—not over the counter, at any rate—but no one drew the line at knives, tridents, clubs, Samurai swords, and fucking maces. The bearded man whom Tim had said was so good at throwing things was inside an armory.

Harry hung outside the third door, hearing nothing unusual going on inside. The man must be near the back, Harry theorized, hoping that Callahan hadn't seen him go in. While he thought out his next move, Harry tried to picture the bearded man with Shanna. He tried to see them in any way, shape, or form. The mental picture did not work. The wild-eyed, bearded man who had to be Jeff Browne looked more suitable throwing knives in a rancid apartment with a corpse on the floor.

Harry calmly walked into the store. He saw Browne in the back corner, ostensibly flipping through a magazine. He had chosen his place well. Although his back was to the door, he had slipped between two other browsers. If Harry had tried to shoot, it would have been a dangerous shot. The only thing Harry could do now was try to get to Browne before the man turned to see if Callahan had passed.

The San Francisco cop moved past the magazine rack to his left and the counter full of signet rings to his right. He walked up three wide steps onto a level with magazine-laden tables on two sides and a cabinet full of blades on the third. He had made it three-quarters of the way toward Browne when the bearded man glanced back.

"Get down!" Harry boomed at the others while he pulled his gun up into full view. Browne wrenched the men beside him in front of the barrel and hurled himself over the counter. One man fell to the ground, but the other froze right in Harry's way. Callahan saw a hand grab a sword off the wall as he pulled the shocked man out of his way.

He blasted two holes in the glass cabinet with the wooden backing. The window section disintegrated and jagged holes appeared in the backing, but Browne would not be flushed out. Harry heard the sword whipping at him before he saw it. He dodged instinctively, but still he was amazed when the blade tore across the tweed at his elbow. Tim had been very right: the guy was very dangerous with knives.

Harry was even more surprised when he heard a cracking blast, and a bullet followed the sword across the room. Even as he threw himself backward across a table, he realized that most of these places usually had a licensed gun on the premises for protection. Naturally, it would be behind the weapons counter, Harry told himself as his shoulder slammed across the slick magazines. You dumb bastard.

Callahan was somersaulting backward. As he felt the edge of the table against his shoulders, he reached down with his free hand and pulled. As he dropped to the floor, the table went with him as a shield. It was a lousy shield, but it would have to do. One way or the other, the gunfight wouldn't last long.

Harry remembered the position of the other counter. He sat up amidst the porno pictures, got his bearings, and shot once through his own table. To his chagrin, there was no return fire. Suddenly, knives began to smash through the tabletop. The bearded man was fighting back, but he was saving his bullets for a final stand.

Harry could only think of one other strategy. If Browne had to conserve his bullets, it made sense that he would think Harry had to do the same. The bearded man could easily count Harry's rounds, since there was a hole in the cabinet backing for every shot. Callahan recalled: Two shots when he came in. Two shots back at the apartment and in the alley. One more through the table. If Browne was counting, he probably thought Harry had one bullet left.

A Samurai sword blade came right through the wood in front of the cop. The hilt stopped the blade inches from his chest. Harry rose up and fired at the head he saw dropping behind the cabinet. His anger nearly did the trick. The shot was perfect. If the Formica and the steel band on the surface of the cabinet hadn't deflected the shot, the lead would have lodged right in Browne's brain.

Instead, the bullet whined, ground, and splattered into the wall behind the bearded man, hacking off some strands of his long curly hair in the process. Then Browne was up and out from his cover, blasting at Harry with a Charter Arms Bulldog .44 Special. Hot damn, Harry thought as he ducked under cover. Those damn guns do get around.

Browne kept firing, running backward toward the door. The gun clicked on an empty chamber, and he nearly fell backward down the three steps at the same time. He twisted in the air, landed with his right foot flat, and then ran for the exit.

Harry had a perfect shot. He stood straight in one smooth motion, clicking open the Magnum's cylinder and dumping the shells out with one hand and pulling a speed loader out of his pocket with another. Callahan always carried four speed loaders—plastic holders that enabled him to load six new rounds in one move.

He swung the cylinder closed with a flick of his wrist as he brought the weapon forward. Once more he had the barrel pointed right in the middle of Browne's back.

And once again, something got in the way. It was the man who had been following him. He had come into the store during the fight and stayed to the side as the bullets flew.

"No!" yelled Tim, putting himself between Browne and the Magnum. "He didn't do anything!"

Callahan bound over the table, took one long step, and charged at the young man, completely bypassing the step. "The hell he didn't," Harry seethed between clenched teeth, bashing the Orenda member out of the way.

Harry raced out into the street again, seeing Browne charge up a stairway one building over. Harry could read a plaque on the stair wall as he approached: "Bishop Hotel: Rooms by the Hour."

"Oh fuck," Harry said, knowing that that was exactly what people were doing upstairs. He pounded up the steps, hearing a gravelly voice shouting above him.

"Hey, what the hell do you think you're doing? Hey, Where're you going! Hey! You can't go in there! Hey!"

At the top of the stairs was a narrow alcove with a beat-up desk, hole-ridden rugs, and a portable TV with a coat hanger for an antenna. In front of it was an old bald man looking up another stairway. His back was to Callahan, and Harry didn't have time to be polite. He pushed the man forward as he jumped. The man fell across the first few steps, Harry's right foot landing on the fifth stair next to the man's head. As he passed, pulling himself up on a banister that nearly cracked with every tug, the deskman's yelling started anew.

There would be no special hiding places for Browne here, Harry knew. Hookers' havens had rooms and that's all. No elevators, no broom closets, and probably no fire escapes. The Fire Department really couldn't care if a bunch of whores got fried, so they probably didn't enforce the regulations much. Only when some crooked chief wanted a payoff did firemen show up at all.

As Harry reached the second level, a door to the left of the hallway smashed open. Harry heard screams as he came up. Inside, he saw Browne barreling through a pile of six women in different costumes. He pushed a nurse aside, tripped a ballerina, knocked over a cheerleader, and jumped across the lying body of a Catholic schoolgirl. A very upset naked man on the bed watched the whole scene.

Harry shot Browne just as he reached a window across the room. The glass was painted black, and it seemed to be part of the wall at first. But when the jacketed semiwadcutter bore into the bearded man's shoulder it propelled him head first through the black crystal.

Light streamed into the room as the girl's screamed and crawled away toward the door. Harry waded through them and looked out the ragged hole. Browne was on his side thirty feet below on a black tar ceiling. He was still alive and moving, though certainly not as fast.

Harry pointed his Magnum again. He centered the barrel this time on Browne's chest. "Halt," he shouted.

The word seemed to mean "Go" to the bearded man. He rolled over onto his stomach and feebly tried to crawl away.

"Hold it," said Harry, tightening his grip on the trigger. Browne kept moving. Callahan nearly shot him again until he remembered what Tim had said. The young man thought Browne was innocent. And he wasn't a raving lunatic like Morrisson. He had faith in and loyalty to Browne. Even after seeing the dead girl in Browne's apartment, Tim was sure the bearded man didn't kill her.

Harry, like everybody else in the Boston Police Department, wanted a fast solution to the case. The chiefs wanted to believe that Morrisson had killed Halliwell and Sherman had killed Morrisson. Harry wanted to believe Collins' theory that Morrisson and Browne were partners. He wanted to believe it because he wanted an easy end. He wanted to get out of Boston. He didn't want to be Linda's confidant or Christine's savior or Collins' best boy. He especially didn't want to be Shanna's protector . . . or judge.

He pulled the gun up. He wasn't going to shoot a helpless man, no matter what he was suspected of. He wouldn't get very far after that fall with a .44 slug in his shoulder. Harry harnessed his Magnum, ignored the bleats of the seven sexually active people around the bed, and went downstairs.

"I called the police!" shouted the deskman as Harry came into view. "I called the police!"

Harry didn't even look at him. He just kept going down the stairs. "No, you didn't," he said as he loped down the remaining steps. The deskman didn't disagree.

Callahan was out on the Combat Zone street for the third time. There was no alley next to the Bishop Hotel, only a strip joint called the Pussy Cat Lounge. Porno men didn't have to think of original names. No one who bought drinks there cared what it was called. Harry went in to find the rear entrance so he could collect Browne. Although it was not yet five o'clock, the place was jumping, at least with music and strippers. "Beautiful, Beautiful Girls Twenty-Four Hours A Day!" the sign in the anteroom promised. The double "Beautiful" may

107

have been an exaggeration, but they weren't kidding about the twenty-four-hour schedule.

As Harry entered the main room, he was assailed by the classic sights of a strip bar. The burly man behind the rectangular bar that filled the foreground. Miserable, stubble-faced men hunching over half-empty glasses. Blaring unidentifiable music, harsh red lighting, and a nearly naked woman who gave new meaning to the word "cellulite."

She was grinding her heels into a runway that stretched back to a door-sized curtain in the rear wall. Harry motioned to the bar man. "Got a rear door in this place?" he yelled over the deep brass and percussion noises.

"Wife after you?" the bartender answered with a slack grin.

Harry pulled out his badge. "That's a Frisco shield!" the barman complained. Harry was impressed with his quick eyes, but didn't want to bandy about jurisdiction. He pulled open his jacket to reveal the Magnum in its holster.

"Right through the curtains at the back," the brawny bar man said immediately. Harry nodded and started in that direction.

The stripper had finished her set. She was making a big deal about her exit. She was building up to a great finish. Just his luck, Harry thought. By the time he got back there, she would be blocking him. He'd either have to wait until she got off or chance touching her. The things he did for a living, he marveled. He held back a bit. Browne would keep. There was no place he could go. The chase was over.

As the thought passed through his mind, someone backstage screamed. Before Harry could act, the stripper about to take the dancer's place fell out from behind the curtains. Browne was holding on to her just to stay up.

The effect was incredible. The spotlights had blasted on to pinion the exiting dancer at the rear portal. They had

108

turned to hot white so the patrons could get a good view of her ripping off her G-string. Instead they spotlighted a frenzied, sweating, bleeding man who was clawing at two girls. Browne lumbered forward like a dying mummy, drooling, crying, and grabbing whatever he could use as a crutch. The strippers tried to pull away, but his fingers had sunk into their arms. When he saw Harry moving up from the side, he kicked the naked woman off the ramp and held the second stripper in front of him.

Harry pulled out his gun. Browne pulled out a knife. Callahan froze when the bearded man jammed it under the stripper's breast. Only a thin Victorian corset separated the steel from her skin.

"Go away, Callahan," Browne hissed slowly. "Can't you see you're making it worse!"

Harry heard the man's words above the roar of the jukebox and the clamor of the customers to get out the door. He glanced in the direction of the noise. He saw the bartender motionless behind the counter, holding a sawed-off shotgun in both hands. He was waiting for his chance. If Harry didn't get the guy, he would.

Callahan looked back at Browne who was painfully edging toward the front door. He couldn't help but feel that he was looking at the real murderer of Judy Halliwell, John Monahan, and Thomas Morrisson. Only a man this obsessive, this possessed, and this driven could have implemented a murder plan like the Orenda one.

"Give up," Harry said tiredly, almost plaintively. "There's nowhere else you can go."

Browne laughed. The laughter cost him. He grimaced in pain, pushing the knife even harder against the stripper's torso. Harry saw the slight material rip. He saw a small stream of blood. "I cut her, didn't I?" said Browne hoarsely. "I cut all the others, too, didn't I? Didn't I?"

His voice was rising to a scream. The stripper knew the right moment when she heard it. She grabbed the knife hand with both of her own, then slammed her stiletto heel on Browne's instep. The bearded man howled in pain. The hardened, experienced girl took the extra second to drive her elbow back right under Browne's septum.

Browne fell off the runway. Harry jumped forward, but the girl, in her panic, was looking back at the bearded man while hurling herself in the opposite direction. She fell right against Harry. It delayed him for a few seconds while the bartender vaulted over the counter.

At that moment, Tim came running in. He shouted, "No!" His hand went up in supplication. In one fist he was holding the empty Bulldog .44 that Browne must have dropped.

The barkeep didn't know the situation. All he saw was another kid waving a gun at him. He swung the shotgun around and let Tim have it with both barrels.

At close range, the scattershot tore right through Tim's chest. His guts splattered against the jukebox a second before his hollow body caught up. His lifeless form smashed through the glass, tearing at the records as he slid down the front. An ear-rending screech filled the room as the tone arm and needle were ripped across the record. Then there was no sound.

Harry moved the stripper out of his way and stepped up onto the runway. The barkeep looked from Tim's corpse to his smoking gun to where Harry stood. The stripper slowly moved around the edge of the stage to look at the spot Browne had fallen. The bartender followed her gaze. They all looked at the place Browne had fallen.

He wasn't there. While Tim was being shot, Browne had crawled to the other side of the bar and gotten away.

Chapter Seven

"This is her car. This is where she was hit on the head. See? That little dent? That little stain? That's where Browne must have slammed her head against the car."

Harry was wondering if Browne hadn't indeed caught him with one of the knives or swords or bullets he threw at him in the porno shop. Because if Callahan had died and gone to hell, this is what Hades would look, sound, and feel like—a gray concrete place with a jolly coroner lecturing while he had a splitting headache.

Callahan nodded, hoping the medical examiner would be magically whisked away by Satan. Instead, the M.E.'s voice was replaced by Collins' cultured, practiced tones.

"Her name was Cathy Bryant. She came from Florida to go to acting school. Her parents said she didn't get into USC or UCLA, and between Carnegie-Mellon in Pittsburgh or Boston University, she chose the lesser of two evils."

"She'd get lung cancer from the smog in Pittsburgh," the coroner mentioned. "She got murdered here." The man tsked-tsked as if it was a hard choice.

"Get him the fuck out of here, will you?" Callahan suggested to the black detective.

"Thanks, Chuck," Collins called to the coroner. "I think we can take it from here."

"All right," the M.E. said a trifle indignantly. Harry

figured he had thus been dismissed on many previous occasions. "All right, already, I'm going. I've got her remains waiting to be examined back at the O.R. anyway. Not that there's much remaining to be examined in the first place. . . ." The coroner's mutter trailed off, echoing in the underground garage.

"I can say this much for him," Collins commented after the M.E. had gone. "He sure loves his work."

"May he become a part of it real soon," Harry blessed him. "This Bryant girl. She wasn't a Unitarian?"

"Never signed up, never helped out, never been there," Collins said. "We showed her picture around the Beacon Street offices. No one remembers her. Besides, her parents said she was Old World Christian."

"Not an Emerson student?"

"BU through and through. Spent her freshman year in the lighting booth. Got some bit parts as a sophomore. Did some repertory work in the chorus. She doesn't even have a friend who goes to Emerson listed in her address book."

Harry looked at the yellow Volvo and the tiny stained dent and realized that was all there was left of a human being. A Boston detective was pouring out all the intimate secrets of her young life, but that stain was all that was really left.

"So why her?" the inspector asked aloud.

It was not the question he really wanted to ask. He really wanted to know "Why not Christine?" And in the very back of his mind he formed the words, "Why not Shanna?" But Collins answered his first query.

"Come on, Harry," the black man said affably. "You know how it is. A guy comes to the end of his rope. Any little thing can set him off. He forgets all about morality. He sees something he wants, and he takes it. All the rules are off. No rhyme. No reason."

It wasn't good enough for Callahan. Something was very wrong. He still couldn't convince himself that

112

Browne had a good enough reason to break the chain. "You show the police sketch in the restaurant?"

Collins sluffed that off. "Sure, but you know how many people come into a restaurant's bar on a busy night. And it had to be at least yesterday when he came in since the girl was snatched this afternoon. Maybe he sat at a table, and she was the only one who really took any notice of him."

"In other words," Callahan translated succinctly, "no one recognizes Browne's picture."

"Nobody has to!" Collins stressed. "He had no classes at the time she was snatched. No one can give him an alibi during the time she was snuffed. No one saw him from the time the girl disappeared to the time you broke into the basement. And there she was, in the middle of the goddamn floor, for Chrissakes! What more could you want?"

Harry wasn't sure, but he still felt something was missing. And Collins' flippant attitude was irritating the hell out of him. He sized the detective up. "You always this callous?"

Collins was unaffected. "Only when it's this open and shut," he admitted happily. "Face it, Harry, we've got our man. All we have to do now is arrest him."

"All you have to do now is find him."

"With a .44-caliber wound in his shoulder and every cop in the city looking, how far could he go?"

"That's what I thought when I first shot him," Harry reminded him.

"Yeah," Collins concurred, coming down from his high a little bit. "Too bad you lost him."

"Yeah," Harry drawled back. "Has any cop in the city found Christine Sherman yet?"

"Your point," Collins conceded. "No, we haven't found her yet. But it's only a matter of time."

"The only problem with that is," Harry lectured, "that it's only a matter of time before Browne finds her, too."

"OK, OK, Inspector," Collins gave in, throwing up his hands. "Ease up on this voice of conscience, will you? I just thought you'd like to tag along and see the Boston PD at work."

Harry leaned up against the Volvo. "It looks like I'm doing all their work for them." He closed his eyes.

"Yeah," Collins laughed. "Right. Speaking of that, Inspector, now that we're alone . . . I thought you might also like to discuss the possible ramifications of the Browne collar."

Callahan opened one eye to see a smiling, expectant black face in front of him. "You're sure blowing a mighty loud horn for a man who hasn't booked the suspect yet."

Collins' suave, worldly facade suddenly fell away to reveal a man totally filled with vengeful joy. "Don't you get it, Harry? I was right! All along I had it all over those pompous lily-asses upstairs, and still they took me off the case. But you proved me right! You caught Browne with his pants down.

"Now this is a noteworthy occasion. This is an important bust for me. But never let it be said that Christopher Collins did not give credit where credit is due. So let's deal, Inspector. What do you want the arrest report to say?"

Harry could no longer keep his amazement to himself. "You get me out of bed at eleven o'clock at night to bring me to some garage graveyard to discuss credit? Whose name goes above the title?"

"Hey, fair is fair," Collins said appeasingly. "I was only trying to be honest about the whole thing, Inspector. I don't know about the SFPD, but there's still a nigger problem here, Mr. Man. Most of the Boston force comes from Southie, otherwise known as South Boston. You may have heard of it. They're the ones who were overturning the school buses full of black children a couple of years ago. I've got to grab hold of every opportunity I can. And this Browne thing is the biggest!"

114

"Look," said Harry, sighing. "Browne is still at large. Sherman is still missing. There are five kids, five goddamn kids and one mother-fucking cat dead, and you want to divvy up the Brownie points?"

Collins backed off. "Hey, look, Inspector, I didn't mean to trample on your sensitivity, but I don't get it. You've blown away more people than that in any given month! You killed your own superior officer once."

"He deserved it," Harry said flatly. "These are kids. Morrisson and Browne. Tim Marchelli, the kid who Browne sicced on me. They're almost teenagers, for Chrissakes."

"Teenagers who raped and murdered," Collins reminded him.

"That isn't proven," Harry shot back.

"What do you want then?" Collins demanded hotly. "A directive from God? What has gotten into you on this case, Callahan?"

Harry didn't answer. He had lost interest in the entire conversation. "I don't know," he finally said, his voice holding more weariness than he had ever heard from it before. "Something's wrong." He got up and moved toward the exit, leaving the last vestige of Cathy Bryant behind. "I'll tell you when I find it."

Harry put his hands in his pockets as he went out into the Brookline Street. A sign said Huntington Avenue. Harry moved due east. It was close to midnight on a Tuesday evening, but the streets were still pretty busy. By the time Harry reached Northeastern University and Symphony Hall, things had quieted down a lot. It was another miserable section of the city—one of Boston's few. Although the concert center was grandly designed, it sat in the middle of a corroding slum. The rolling, buckling streets were littered with cans, glass, and McDonald's wrappers.

Harry turned left and went up Massachusetts Avenue. He knew if he kept walking north along that road, he would cross the Charles River into Cambridge, home of

115

M.I.T. and Harvard. Harry didn't go that far. As he passed a squat apartment building on the left, an incredibly majestic, incredibly large building rose on his right.

It was a magnificent cathedral, flanked by a marble, monolithic building, all built around a huge, flat reflection pool. The complex seemed dropped in. It was an oasis of architectual magnificence in a section of abject poverty.

That was Boston all over, Callahan thought as he traversed the beautifully built square. On the surface, it was clean, calm, and serene. The many colleges rolled on and the many stores existed off the students. It was a university town made up of over two hundred educational facilities. But just under the surface, corruption bubbled. There were dank, evil things that waited in pockets of gloom all over the city. Waiting. Just waiting for someone to take the wrong step.

Beyond the religious-looking square, things got better, and Harry's mood lifted somewhat. He walked up the back stairs to the Prudential Building, once the highest skyscraper in Boston. He walked around the closed-up building, which looked like a giant three-dimensional computer card, into another square built at the front.

By then, the city seemed devoid of life. There was a statue of a muscular God in front of Harry as he looked out to see a sign that identified the road in front of the insurance building as Tremont Street. Callahan may have imagined that Boston was a subtly insidious city, but it was also a close-knit one. He had walked almost to the intersection where Collins had driven him that first morning.

As he thought of Collins, he saw two uniformed policemen walking below him. They were chatting pleasantly, secure in the knowledge that the beat was at its daily quietest. He heard the men talking.

"The Pru is still here," said a baby-faced one.

"Hey, you ever been to the restaurant on the top floor?" asked his partner, a man with a mustache.

"Yeah. Took my wife there once."

"You know what they call it?"

"Sure. Top of the Pru. Why?"

"Well," said the mustached cop. "They were thinking of building a restaurant just like it in that new insurance building down the street."

"What, the Hancock Building?" asked Baby-face incredulously. "They only built that to be taller than this one. And it hasn't settled yet!"

"Still. They want to open a restaurant on the very last floor. And you know what they're calling it?"

Both men said it at once. "The Top of the Cock!" The mustached one cracked up. The baby-faced one smirked and nodded his head. He had heard it before.

Harry hadn't. He grinned, as much at the rotten joke as at the pair's comaraderie. They had moved past the statue and the fountain in front of it to walk through a splash of light coming through a storefront that Harry couldn't see.

As he watched, Baby-face slapped Mustache's arm. The two looked in through the window out of Harry's sight line. Then they went for their guns and ran forward.

The window blew outward, taking Mustache with it. Harry saw it just before he heard the familiar boom of a sawed-off shotgun. The mustached cop went down on the wide sidewalk among hundreds of spinning glass globes. He landed on his back and blood squished out onto the pavement around his torso in a halo effect. His gun clattered across the concrete and dropped off the curb.

Baby-face was returning fire even before his dead partner's gun had hit the street. He ducked just before there was another boom. Harry was taking the steps down to the street three at a time. He wrenched out the Magnum as the baby-faced cop tried to run for cover. A car screeched around the closest corner and jumped the curb. It barreled right for Baby-face, smashing aside a row of

117

shopping carts and a bicycle rack as it went. The cop emptied his service revolver at the oncoming leviathon, but his .38 bullets didn't even slow it down.

Callahan strode out onto the wide walkway ten feet behind the petrified cop. With one quick shot he blew out the big car's front left tire.

Baby-face didn't hear the roar of Harry's cannon. All he knew was that the auto had suddenly lifted up on one side and was swerving away from him. But the danger wasn't over. The vehicle was still barreling while turning increasingly sideways. The cop ran to the right and threw himself forward just as the rear of the car swung by him. Harry saw the rear bumber skim the small of Baby-face's back.

Then the car turned completely around and screeched to a halt, facing in the opposite direction. The lone driver screamed out his side and started shooting out the passenger window at the crouching cop.

"Come on!" the driver screeched. "Let's go!"

No one had seen Harry yet. He ran out even farther from the building's side to see the shattered storefront of a twenty-four-hour Star Market. Inside were two men hauling money-filled cases and several employees as well as patrons lying on the tile floors.

Baby-face was caught in a cross fire. He was out in the middle of the sidewalk with an empty gun while the crooks inside the store were shooting at him and the driver was pumping lead through the car's side window.

Harry shot the driver in the back of the head through the rear window just as the man stepped on the gas again. The .44 slug ripped through the heavy car glass and drilled into the driver's head. The front of the man's face came off and spread across the front windshield. His leg muscles spasmed, pushing the accelerator to the floor.

The car sped forward, the flat tire dragging it sideways again, half-off and half-on the sidewalk. It slammed broadside against a newspaper machine, caught the undersides of two side tires then started flipping down the street. It barrel-rolled five times before crashing into a line of parked cars. It flipped high over them, its hood and trunk flapping open, then came down on its roof, crushing the two vehicles beneath it. The night was cracked by the splitting whump of four more tires exploding out.

The baby-faced cop looked down the street at the devastated cars. He should have been looking behind him. As Harry ran around to the front of the store, one of the ski-masked men inside shot Baby-face in the back. Harry shot the robber back. The cop fell forward, his eyes still open. The robber flew backward, his arms flailing in the air, his .45 Army automatic flying into the fresh fruit department.

The last man ripped off his ski mask to get a clear look at what was going on. He followed his fellow robber's trajectory as the already dead crook arced over a bagging table and fell on top of a cash register. The machine rang and the money drawer popped out.

The man shot wildly out the front window at the fast-moving, shadowy form and ran toward the back of the store. Harry came into the light and leaped through the shotgun-shattered front window, the Magnum smoking. He jumped up on one of the cashier counters and followed the last robber into the body of the store.

He ran across the front of the aisles to locate his quarry. He caught him speeding down aisle seven. He aimed and fired the .44 just as the man threw himself across the meat counter that stretched all the way across the rear wall. Harry's slug dug into a shoulder roast, sending out little hunks of plastic and raw meat.

The robber popped up from behind the counter and sprayed the aisle with .45 rounds. Bottles of grapefruit, grape, orange, and apple juice exploded out, and liquid bled across the rows. Harry threw himself against a stack of Saltines, still moving into aisle six. He ran all the way

119

down to the side of the store and the bread department where the meat counter in the back ended. The robber couldn't get a bead on him there.

He ran to the rear of the store just in time to see the last man pushing through two swinging doors into the refrigerated meat section of the market. Harry vaulted the meat counter and went after him. The man spun with his back against the conveyor belt which brought the cut, wrapped, and marked meat out to the counter. Both men's breath appeared as frosty clouds in front of their faces. Harry's face was misting. The robber's face was pumping out clouds of white fog.

He pulled up his automatic on a level with Harry's chest. Harry brought up his own gun. The robber, at the same time, tried to steady himself with his other hand. A mistake. He put his palm on the red-hot machine that seals plastic wrap around meat. His skin was melted instantly. He screamed in pain, his other arm jerked and the Army automatic boomed.

Harry shot at the same time. Cooly, steadily, with two hands. The robber's bullet whined off the concrete ceiling and metal supports. Harry's lead punched into the man's chest just under his neck.

His torso was thrown back, his feet slid across the icy floor and swung up. His hand remained seared to the plastic-stapler machine. The robber landed heavily on the conveyor belt, the stench of burning flesh beginning to fill the air. The .45 rolled out through a flapping door and onto the meat counter.

Harry approached slowly. Blood was soaking through the man's jacket as the belt tried to bring him outside, but his stuck hand was making him stay. He looked at Callahan through drooping eyelids. There was a flash of recognition.

"Cops," the robber said disgustedly. "They're never what they seem." Then he died.

Harry pried the man's hand off the plastic-sealer and dropped the corpse on the meat-packing floor. If the cops didn't find him, the store butchers would know what to do with him later in the morning.

Harry was brought into the manager's office by a grateful cashier. He called the police and asked for Collins.

"Come over to the Star Market on Tremont," Harry suggested when the detective came on. "Now *I* have a mess for *you t*o clean up."

It was almost four-thirty in the morning before Harry got back to the Holiday Inn. He was lucky. If Collins hadn't been there to pave the way for his quick release, it would have been questions, forms, and detention until at least Wednesday afternoon. As it was, Harry did a swan dive onto the hotel room's bed and slept until ten.

They say that murderers have nightmares. They say that people who are twisted and sick often have subconsciouses that run wild while they sleep. Many say that is a reason that all the weirdos prowl the night. They don't want to sleep. They don't want to look at themselves.

They say that killers don't have nightmares. They might dream about this or that, but their visions don't dredge up horrible scenes of gore. They say it is because the people who deliberately kill know what they're doing and why they're doing it. They are not expending personal desires or fulfilling a blood lust. If they must kill, they do, and it doesn't fester.

Callahan didn't dream. There were no visions of melting hands or bleeding strippers or Christine's pleading face at the bottom of a well filled with blood. These visions tickled Harry's mind when he awoke, not when he was safe at rest.

First thing he did was call room service. He ordered parts of nearly every breakfast. He knew it would take a while, so he showered, shaved, changed into a brown suit, and called Collins.

"Nothing to report, O Lord High Executioner," the black man cracked, referring to Harry's shooting spree of the previous night. Nowhere in Collins' voice was there

121

any evidence of the tense talk they had had in the Brookline parking garage. Callahan suddenly remembered the last robber's last words. "Cops are never what they seem."

Emptying his mind of memories for the moment, Harry heard that Browne had not been run to ground yet, that the Sherman girl had not been seen, and that otherwise everything was all right with God and country. Harry hung up. Everything might be right in Collins' world, he thought, but the sword still hung over the Donovan family.

Harry had to push things along. He had to be sure of what Shanna was and who's side she was on. Was she an innocent bystander, a possible victim, or a knowing accomplice? There was a knock on the door. Callahan decided not to find out until after breakfast.

Ten hours after Harry had hit the sack, he was hitting the road again. The sky was getting a bit bleak—gray clouds wisping overhead—but Harry liked it that way. The cloud cover brought out the other colors of the city all the more forcefully. Everything was sharp and outlined against the dull background tapestry. There was a comfortable feeling of moisture in the air that wasn't clammy but crisp.

Normally, it would have lifted the inspector's spirits. He had beaten a gang of crooks, there was no one tailing him, and Collins was positive the Beacon Hill Murders case was coming to a close. But among those robbers' bodies were the corpses of two cops. The insides of the man who had been tailing Harry were still being sopped up off the floor of the Pussy Cat Lounge, and there were still some annoying inconsistencies nagging Callahan about the Orenda case.

He mulled it over in his mind without success while he trudged toward Shanna's apartment. Nothing was coherent by the time he arrived at the handsome corner building placed among many others between Charles Street and Storrow Drive. He walked around the iron grillwork of the banister wall and trotted down the five steps to Shanna's thick basement-apartment door. He knocked sharply.

"Just a second, babe," he heard her voice immediately call. He heard the deadbolt unlocking and the chain being thrown off. Then the heavy, windowless portal swung back. Shanna was positively beaming in the doorway, wearing only a thin, designed shirt tied just under her almost exposed breasts and a pair of lace panties. When she saw who was standing there, her jaw nearly dropped to the level of her belly button.

"H-Harry!" she attempted to recover, gulping.

"Hello," he said, unsmilingly surveying her handsome limbs. "Expecting someone?"

Shanna wasn't as polished a liar as Harry had become. If the positions were reversed, Harry would have said yes. That would've given him more time to think of a decent excuse. And if he couldn't think of one and the questioner was rude enough to ask who, he could've said "none of your damn business." Of course, Harry would look ridiculous in Shanna's outfit though.

Shanna was acting none too comfortable in it either. Normally, she may have responded with aggression to Harry's question, but Callahan was not her parents. He was still a veritable stranger. Quickly, nervously, Shanna replied, "No." An obvious lie.

It only made things worse, and both of them knew it. If Shanna was covering for someone and uncovering herself for that same someone, it was natural for Harry to assume that she was waiting for her lover, Jeff Browne.

"Hey, listen," she said, trying to recover, "come on in while I finish dressing."

"Thanks," Harry said, ducking slightly and entering. It was a cozy place, basically structured in a hexagon. There was a little bathroom to the left of the door, a little kitchen across the way, and Shanna's bed to the right. She had decorated it nimbly, highlighting the two windows high on the wall and the rustic, "study-like" feeling of the place. Harry would've felt comfortable here if the tension wasn't so strong.

Shanna skipped over to a bureau and a steamer trunk next to the bed. She quickly pulled out a dark jacket and a pair of jeans. She seemed expectant, waiting for Harry to pursue the matter of her greeting outfit. Harry didn't. He had already reached a theory. He merely waited for corroborating evidence.

Shanna sat on the bed and pulled the denims over her underwear. "Hope I didn't shock you," she said with forced flippancy. "I'm usually never visited by anybody except friends and they all know what I'm like. I just like to feel comfortable, you know? Clothes give me a bound-in feeling."

Harry had to admit it was good. And it probably had some basis in fact. But combining her lack of clothing with her call when he knocked added up to the arrival of an anticipated guest. Shanna didn't call just anybody "babe."

She undid the knot in the shirt, quickly buttoned it and stuck it down the waistband of her pants. She zipped them up the shrugged the jacket on. "Hey," she continued. "I have to go out anyway. I told Dr. Gerrold I might be stopping by." She pulled a pair of boots out from beneath the bed.

Harry just watched her from his standing position near the door. "Tom Morrisson is dead," he said.

Shanna looked up and blinked. "What?"

"Christine Sherman is missing. I found the body of a Brookline waitress in Jeff Browne's apartment. Jeff stabbed a girl downtown, and I shot him in the shoulder. He got away but not before Tim Marchelli died."

Shanna stared at Harry open-mouthed.

"The police think that Christine killed Tom in self-defense and is hiding out in shock and fear. I'm not so sure. I think Browne may have killed Morrisson so he couldn't talk and taken Christine with him. I'm afraid she might already be dead as well."

"Harry," Shanna breathed in astonishment. "What are you saying?"

"You're in over your head, Shanna," he answered in the same flat tone of voice he had rattled off the body count in. "Browne is using you at the very best. At the very worst, he's planning to kill you next."

"What are you talking about?" Shanna repeated explosively. "Jeff wouldn't kill me!"

"The police think he killed Judy Halliwell and that other boy as well," Harry went on. "I'm afraid they may be right."

Her reaction was unusual. She stared at Harry, first in wonder, then in confusion, and finally in anger. She reached down and jammed on her other boot. "I don't want to hear this," she said, more irritated then frightened. She strode over to the desk near the door and scooped up her keys. "Listen," she said to Harry's face. "You can believe whatever you like but I'm not going to stand here and listen to that bullshit." She headed for the door, passing Harry by. "Stay as long as you like," she snapped at him flippantly.

She had just turned the knob when Harry's hand gripped her arm. Almost effortlessly, he pulled her back and threw her onto the bed.

"It makes no difference if you believe it," he said evenly. "It makes no difference if I believe it. The fact is people are being murdered. People you know. People who are close to you. You can make believe it doesn't effect you or concern you, but you're only fooling yourself. You are in danger."

"I'm in danger every day on the street," Shanna countered hotly. "I get the looks, I get the leers. I've had to change my number three times because the same obscene caller keeps getting it. I get pornographic notes in my school box. Haven't you read the papers, Harry? Haven't you heard? It's open season on girls. We've surpassed deers as the favorite hunting prize. Girls are getting raped, kidnapped, and murdered all the time. What's so different about today?"

She didn't have to tell Harry. Pictures of every San Francisco girl who got croaked passed his desk. "The difference," he informed her, "is today somebody's out there who isn't going to hit on the first girl who strikes his fancy. He's looking for you. He's after you."

Shanna accepted the information silently. Then she leaned back, looked at the ceiling, and laughed without mirth. "Christ," she said. "Jesus Christ. I'm just about to get my act together, and this has to happen." She looked back down at her relative. "Look, Harry," she said calmly. "Thanks for your concern, but I'm all right. I'm perfectly safe. I'm in no more danger than I usually am. Jeff isn't going to come after me. If he was going to come after me, why kill that blonde waitress?"

Harry had a reason for that as well. But it was a reason he wasn't going to say right out. Not until he had better evidence.

"Can't you see you're making it worse?" Shanna pleaded. "Everything was fine, it was really getting better until you showed up. Mom sends you flying in like Superman and the Lone Ranger all wrapped into one, and everything just starts falling apart." She looked at the digital clock-radio by her bed. "Jeez, I really have to get to my counselor's office. I said I'd stop by."

"I'll walk you," said Harry.

"No, don't," said Shanna quickly. "I don't want you to," she went on with equal conviction. She stepped up to him demurely. She put the flat of her hands against his chest and looked up into his eyes. "Look, Harry, I really love you, but leave it alone. It will all take care of itself, I promise. You won't help anything by getting involved."

She looked at him imploringly. He simply looked back without a change of expression. She dropped her hands and left the apartment, leaving the door open after her.

Harry walked to the entrance and watched her go. She kept her head up and didn't look back.

"You're only making it worse," he remembered. There was an echo in his mind. Jeff Browne had said it to him while he held a knife against a stripper's chest, and Shanna just said it. There were two minds that thought alike.

Harry couldn't bring himself to believe that those two minds thought alike in more ways than that. Shanna wanted to know why Browne didn't kill her before the Brookline waitress. She had a point. Harry asked himself again. "Why not Shanna?" This time he answered. "Because maybe Browne never had any intention of murdering Shanna. Maybe Shanna wasn't even a target." And Harry could only think of one reason that could be.

Harry tried picturing Shanna up on a Beacon Hill rooftop, holding a knife against Judy Halliwell's throat as Browne raped her. He tried to see her holding Christine back while Browne killed Morrisson. He tried to see her helping Browne to drag Cathy Bryant to another car.

It was a sign of just how long Harry had been a cop when he was able to realistically picture Shanna as a murderer's accomplice. He was able to do it real easy.

Chapter Eight

Harry Callahan returned to the Holiday Inn at one o'clock in the morning. He had spent ten hours trailing his red-headed relative. She had gone to Gerrold's Newbury Street office as she said she would and spent an hour there. Then she went to the library, stopped at a store to buy a pair of "No Nonsense" pantyhose, got back to the Emerson cafeteria at 150 Beacon Street to have some dinner, went home for some homework, returned to 130 Beacon Street to do some remixing on a friend's film project, went out for a drink in Copley Square with the friend, then went home again and to bed.

Harry had seen neither hide nor hair of Jeff Browne. He may have been scared away from their rendezvous by spotting Harry at the apartment. It was vaguely possible that he had cut off his beard and slipped her a note among the library racks or in the crowded dining hall, but Callahan doubted it. He considered himself a better detective than to let them get away with something like that.

But that happily married man in the back of his mind said that Shanna could've been telling the truth. The "uncle" who had bounced her on his knees an era ago whispered that she was still guileless, still innocent. Harry wasn't going to decide one way or the other. He'd let reality dictate the truth to him. In the meantime, he'd just keep watching and digging.

Callahan approached the night clerk. "Any messages for me?" he asked. The man checked his room box.

"No, sir."

Harry went upstairs. When he entered his room, he saw the little red message light on the phone blinking even before he turned on the other illumination. Still without switching on the light, Harry angrily pulled the receiver to his ear and dialed the front desk.

"This is room 2125," he said when the desk answered. "I just left the lobby. I thought you said there were no calls for me."

"Oh yes, sir," said the man. "There were several calls for you, but no messages."

Harry closed his eyes. "Just a second," he said. "I think there's something wrong with our connection." Then he slammed the mouthpiece against the edge of the bed table, hard. He hung up before the deskman could wail in pain.

He returned to the door and switched on the lights. Then he saw the envelope under his foot. It was a letter. From Jeff Browne.

The pale white light globes that dotted the Boston Common were the only illumination that streaked the front of the Unitarian Headquarters building. The gray clouds that had been threatening the ground with moisture all day had covered the moon, as well as finally releasing patches of intermittent drizzle.

All of Beacon Hill had a slick, glossy, wet-down look. Harry looked back up Joy Street. The road seemed to end at the top of the hill, then all there was was sky, framed by the townhouses at the very apex. Harry looked back toward Beacon Street. The Common was empty as far as he could see. He poked his head around the left corner. The sidewalk in front of the Church offices was clear.

He checked his watch. It was three A.M., the exact time

the letter had said Jeff would meet him. It was a hastily scrawled ink letter on plain lined paper. It looked like it had been torn from a school composition book.

"The police are on a vendetta against the Orenda. If they catch me, they will kill me. I want to stop. I have to stop. If you meet me, I will give myself up. But no police. I still have Christine. If there are cops there, I will take her with me."

It was all very clever. At no time did Browne admit to killing anyone. He did not openly threaten Christine. He only professed to having a paranoia complex and a desire to stop. Once they got him in a station house, he might very well say that he had been referring to the heartbreak of psoriasis all along. Perverted mass murderers were getting very crafty in this age of plea bargaining and cushy insane asylums.

Harry moved cautiously out onto Beacon Street. The large block letters, "T-R-A-P," kept flashing across his consciousness like the light-bulb signs on the bottom of the Goodyear Blimp. He acknowledged to himself that if there was an ambush, Shanna might be in on it. He slowly reached into his jacket to grip the handle of the Magnum. He prepared himself to shoot her if he had to.

He got as far as the Unitarian entranceway without being mowed down. He felt a drop of rain on his forehead. He was wound so tight, he nearly jerked his head to the side because of it. Then more raindrops fell. He could still see no one approaching the door from any direction, so he moved up the steps out of the drizzle.

He looked at the door and did a double take. There was a thin line of light coming from the space at the bottom of the portal. Harry jumped lightly over the rest of the steps. He tried the knob. It was open.

Harry jumped back to the street and raced around the corner as fast as he could. He ran to the back of the building, leaped onto a stone wall with a high metal fence attached to it, vaulted over the top of the steel-poled obstruction, and charged at the first window he saw.

131

As he ran, he pulled off his jacket and wrapped it around one arm, as if he were going to face an attack dog. Harry threw himself sideways at the window. He held his jacket-wrapped arm in front of his face. The glass and wooden framing gave way like rice paper under his speeding bulk. He saw the wooden slats of the floor seemingly moving under his feet. He felt himself begin to drop just as the glass shards started smashing all around him. He pushed his bent knees straight. He landed flat, balanced, and kept on going.

He threw the jacket off his arm as he reached for the darkened room's doorknob. With his other hand, he got the gun loose. When he pulled open the portal and charged into the foyer the Magnum was cocked and ready.

Browne was caught by surprise. As Harry had thought, the bearded man was just inside the front door, waiting for him to walk right into a knife. Browne instantly whirled about as Harry came through the back way. Then the bearded man crouched behind another figure that was kneeling on the ground in front of him.

It was Christine Sherman. Although the lower half of her face was almost completely covered by a Western kerchief, Harry had no trouble recognizing her. Her eyes were half-closed and her head sagged as if she were drugged. Her arms had been cruelly bound behind her with thin rope. A coarse wooden pole had been placed against her back and the ropes that were wrapped around her wrists, elbows, and upper arms had been tied to that as well, effectively keeping her back straight.

Her kneeling form was covered with Indian clothing. Animal skins covered her shoulders and bent legs. A mantle was covering her back. Around her neck and down her chest she was wearing thick circles of beads and several silver brooches. A bead wampum belt was tied around her waist. Other than that, she was naked.

Harry moved forward toward them.

"Hold," he heard Browne hiss. He had a long ceremonial knife pressed against her neck. It had a two-sided copper blade and a wooden wolf's head carved in the handle. "You come any closer and she shall meet the wolf," the bearded man said slowly, almost torturedly.

Harry could have pegged him if any bit of vulnerable skin was above Christine's kneeling form. But the pole attached to her wrists and again to her neck by one thin leather thong was making her an effective shield.

"I thought you said you were giving up," Harry said.

"No," came the slow, precise voice again. "You are like the rest. You killed all the Indians and stole all their land. You broke every treaty with the red man. You will lie and kill me, too."

"Come on, Browne," Harry said in astonishment. "Why would I kill you now? Just come out without the knives."

The bearded man didn't answer. Instead, Christine began to rise. Browne was lifting her up. A single blanket was knotted around her waist. Harry could see where the two ends overlapped that her legs were not tied. The bearded man pulled her backward toward the door.

"Don't follow or I'll kill you." Browne edged out the open door, keeping Christine fully in front of him at all times. She followed him like a sleepwalker.

As soon as they were completely out the door, Harry raced forward, spun around at the last minute, and ran up the staircase. He kept going until he reached the top floor. He raced from room to room until he found the door to the roof. It was locked shut. He kicked it open. Only thirty seconds had passed since Browne had escaped. Harry hoped he wasn't too late.

He ran to the Beacon Street side first. If Browne had a car, he could spot it, report it, and join Collins on the hunt. He looked down. No parked car had moved. They all sat in the same line they had when Harry had first appeared that evening.

He ran to the Joy Street side. It was the second most logical escape route. The other direction simply held the

133

business district near Government Center. Deeper into Beacon Hill there were alleys and cellars and empty apartments and many other places to hide. Callahan spotted them right away. Browne was dragging the bound-and-gagged girl up the street.

Harry considered trying to nail him at that distance but thought better of it. In the rainy night and with both killer and victim so far gone, it would be too risky. Harry couldn't afford to let Browne know he was still on the trail until he had him at point-blank range. He couldn't give Browne a chance to slice the girl in retaliation.

There was a fire escape on the same side of the building. Harry hopped over the edge and dashed down the metal stairway as quickly and quietly as he could. By the time he landed on Joy Street again, his shirt was stuck to his skin, and the rest of his clothes were sodden. The escaping pair had disappeared over the top of the hill.

Harry trotted after, pulling the Magnum again from its berth. Even in this situation, even though Browne was obviously out of his mind and was still recovering from a bullet wound, Harry didn't trust him not to get away. Both Callahan and Collins had been sure they had him at one time or another, and in both instances Browne had eluded them. The Orenda head had the strength and the cunning of the homicidally insane.

Harry got to the top of the hill. The two had effectively vanished. Stretched out in front of Callahan was the rest of Beacon Hill, a half-dozen different streets running in every direction. The cop was about to curse and start a fast reconnaissance when he saw a blanket resting across the sidewalk of an intersection.

Browne had made a mistake. He was crazy enough and possessed enough to dress Christine in ceremonial gear, but she was conscious enough and aware enough to use the various pieces like bread crumbs to lead Harry on. Callahan ran to the fallen mantle. It stretched from the curb of Joy Street to the curb of a bisecting road.

Harry looked down the new way. Like all the other

streets on Beacon Hill, it was sloping steeply, lined with rustic brownstones and dotted with old-fashioned street lamps. Harry peered through the rain, seeing the river and Cambridge in the misty distance. He ran in that direction until he saw another animal skin lying in the middle of another road to the right.

A final skin was lying against the curb alongside a fence. The fence was covered with graffitti. Harry studied all the streets in every direction. There was not a sign of any other Indian equipment in any direction. He studied the fence. It seemed solid. He began to move cautiously along its slats, looking for some kind of opening.

His toe had just touched the skin lying against the end of the fence when he heard the scream. It was a gurgling, choked cry, but it was loud enough for Harry to realize that it was coming from the other side of the fence.

Callahan moved back quickly. He didn't shoot through the slats in case Christine was still in the way. He prepared himself to break through or climb over the obstruction. Just as he hunched, a small metallic clatter followed the shriek, and then there was an easily recognizable boom. Harry didn't have to see a chunk of the fence spin away to know Browne had gotten his hands on another gun.

In his condition, Harry couldn't allow Browne to go any further. Harry had seen others like him. They would kill their hostages, then, if they couldn't get the cops, they would kill themselves. He had to risk jumping the fence blind.

The fence was too high to vault. He'd have to handle it like a gymnast's horse. He slid the gun into the holster, ran, jumped, and grabbed the top edge with both hands. He hauled his torso up until his waist slapped against the top. In this position, for this split second, he was a sitting duck.

In that split second he saw why he wasn't dead. Christine seemed fully awake and was fighting Browne with all her might. She had worked the kerchief off her face to reveal a thick cloth knotted between her teeth, holding a sponge in her mouth. The rain had dampened it so much that she had been able to condense it enough to cry out. Her legs were kicking out at the bearded man, who clutched at his shoulder and seemed confused. Christine's hair was plastered to her head in dripping wet corkscrews. Her nose was bleeding down into the sponge. Her arms were still held fast behind her back with the rope. Other than that hemp and the Indian necklaces, she was naked in the cold rain.

Harry pulled his legs up and to the side. They passed over the fence, and he dropped to his feet. He noticed a carefully constructed latch and two hinges on the inside of the fence. It was a concealed door.

Browne and Christine were struggling in the middle of a small playground. As Harry was able to point his gun again, Christine was able to break away from the bearded man. He swung at her with his knife, but she was too fast. The tip of the blade just missed her head as she fell forward at Harry's feet.

Callahan finally had him. Browne's chest was practically filling his vision. His Magnum was aimed right at the bearded man's heart with nothing in the way.

Harry didn't shoot. Not because he pitied Browne. Not because he was beneath contempt. Not because it wouldn't be worth it. Something was wrong.

Browne just stood there, a knife in one hand, a snub-nosed revolver in the other. He held them both out away from his body. They weren't pointing at anyone.

The bearded face looked bewildered. There wasn't just rain pouring down his face. There was sweat. Harry could see him shivering. And it was from more than the cold somehow.

"All right, Browne," Harry said. "That's it." He reached back behind him and swung open the playground door. Keeping his Magnum steady on the bearded man's chest, he leaned down to help Christine up. He moved her toward the exit, watching Browne every second.

The bearded man didn't move. He didn't try to kill either of them. His face still seemed disconcertingly muddled, as if he were listening to an argument in his head.

"No more sacrifices, Jeff," Harry coaxed. "Put the stuff down and let's get out of the rain."

The eyes that had been looking through Harry suddenly focused on him. Then they grew wild, hysterical. Browne's whole body began to shake with violent spasms. The knife fell out of his hand. He grabbed the snub-nose in both and started screeching in short, sharp pants.

Harry kept the Magnum centered on his chest with both his hands. He pursed his lips, waiting for the first sign that Browne was going to shoot. He didn't have long to wait.

The bearded man fell to one knee and pointed the pistol straight out in front of him. Even at the last, Harry couldn't bring himself to shoot him again. He fell and rolled to the side, fully prepared to peg him if it was the only way to stay alive. He heard a gun go off, but it was a distant, muffled sound. He came up in a crouch in time to see Browne fall back.

The bearded man hit the sodden playground dirt with a tiny splash, the gun still clutched in his hand.

Harry turned. Christine was rubbing her back against the side of the wooden door, desperately trying to push the sponge out from behind the knotted cloth so she could tell him what had happened. In a few seconds, she didn't have to. Detective Christopher Collins walked through the playground door, his Smith and Wesson .38 Model 10 clutched in his right hand.

Callahan glared at him in angry amazement.

"You were acting strange," Collins told him before either of them made a move toward the bound girl or the motionless body. "I, uh, was worried about you, you know? Thought you might be able to use a back up, a guardian angel." He looked pointedly at Browne's body. "Looks like I was just in time, huh?"

Harry just kept glaring. The black detective finally

looked away and went to make sure Browne was really dead.

The press conference was a huge success. In other words it was another in a long line of First Amendment fiascos. The reporters poured into the Justice Building, which was just down the street from the Prudential and Hancock buildings, to watch a police promotion and see the beautiful survivor of the "Beacon Hill Murders."

Hot lights, cameras, and microphones were shoved in Christine's face. But rather than shrink behind Harry, she just shone back. She smiled radiantly, answered questions with breathy sincerity and generally did her best to be a noble, brave, honest little trooper.

Collins was used to the scene but his policemanese was even sharper since he was the center of attraction. "Alleged perpetrators," "stake-outs," and other famous cop phrases were littering the air like pages of a Jack Webb script. It was just what the members of the press wanted. They lapped it up like starving dogs.

Harry scowled throughout the whole ceremony. But on his face a scowl looked fairly natural—even attractive. Not that many of the reporters noticed it. Their concentration was on the "beautiful brunette who survived the terrifying ordeal," and the "brave black detective from the slums of the Roxbury section who came to the Big City Police Department to make good." Harry was merely a "visiting Frisco Inspector who assisted in the arrest."

Even if they had filmed his dour expression, they could not have possibly captured the taste of ashes in his mouth. Christine had gotten a lot of attention, and Collins had gotten a lot of glory, but the case still stunk. The whole thing was still a jumbled mess in Callahan's mind. It just served to cap his feelings about the Boston "vacation." It was Thursday morning and Harry figured he'd head back to San Fran a day early.

It made no difference, he thought. The killer was dead.

Shanna didn't have anything to do with it. It was time to kiss everybody off and hope they never wrote him again. Harry left the room as soon as the last decoration was pinned to Collins' chest and the last close-up of Christine's serenely gorgeous face was taken.

Collins broke away from the many clutching, congratulating hands to catch up with him in the hall.

"Hey, Inspector," he called, "aren't you sticking around? I figure I owe you at least a celebration dinner. Hell, I'll take you, Christine, *and* Shanna to Pier Four, the most popular restaurant in the world."

Harry spun toward him as if the black man had tapped him with a cattle prod. "You used me," Callahan seethed. "You used me from moment one."

"Hey, hey, Harry," Collins backed off, his hands up. "I only did what I had to to solve the case."

"You knew I had family here," Harry snarled. "But you played dumb. Why?"

"It wasn't hard to figure out," Collins shrugged. "We checked all the Unitarian volunteers thoroughly in the first place. Shanna Donovan, daughter of Peter and Linda Donovan, mother's maiden name Callahan. Then you just happen to show up right outside the offices at an opportune moment? Come on, now. Really."

"So why not level with me? Why have me stumbling around in the dark?"

"I *did* level with you, Harry," the black man maintained. "I didn't lie to you once. Everything I said about the chiefs taking me off the case was true. But I looked you up. I found out your rep. 'Dirty Harry.' I figured you'd be more capable of cutting through all the bullshit than I would. Especially considering your personal stake in the matter."

Harry pushed him against the wall. Once. Hard. Then he just looked at him.

"Give me a break, will you, Callahan?" Collins complained, straightening his dress uniform. "Don't tell me you wouldn't have done the same thing in my position."

Harry didn't bother. The black man was so starry-eyed from his moment of glory he wouldn't have been able to understand that he had stepped on Harry to get ahead. That he had not only used Callahan but the deaths of everyone along the way to climb the police ranks. He didn't care about the victims. He didn't care about the murderer. All he cared about was himself.

Harry wished he could spit out all the bile he felt inside him into Collins' face. Instead he turned silently and headed for the exit. He felt a tug on his sleeve just as he got to the door. He nearly whirled around and lashed out. Instead he turned slowly. Christine Sherman had run after him this time. She hugged him before he could do or say anything more. Then she kissed him.

"Aren't you staying?" she asked brightly, holding onto his arms while leaning back.

He held her up by the hips. "It's been a long few days," he said apologetically. "I've still got a job in San Francisco."

"You mean you're going back tonight?" Christine asked incredulously.

Harry was sorely tempted to say no. The girl was wearing a wraparound dress that did even more for her than the designer jeans. But in her eyes, Harry could see parts of the last week. Parts he would sooner forget. "I'm afraid so," he finally answered.

Christine's full lips turned down into a practiced pout. "Are you sure?" she asked, fully aware of her effect on men.

Harry sighed, looked up at the ceiling, and grinned. His only answer was a helpless shrug.

Christine knew she had made progress. "Well," she drawled. "Just in case your plane is leaving a little late, here's my address." She handed him an already made-out scrap of paper.

Harry put it in his jacket pocket. "Just in case the plane's late," he agreed.

Then she gave him something to remember her by as

well as a promise of things to come. The kiss, this time, was long and serious. She broke away, moving back down the hall way slowly, luxuriously. "See you later," she said with complete assurance.

On the way to the hotel, Callahan marveled at her rapid recovery from the "terrifying ordeal." Well, why not, he told himself. She was unconscious half the time. As far as he could tell and as far as she had said in her statement, Browne had kept her so high on peyote all the time she hadn't known whether she was asleep or awake.

The sun was out on this Thursday morning. Boston seemed to be moving again after the announcement that the "Beacon Hill Murderer" was no more. Ah, what the hell, Harry figured, shaking off the remnants of the case. It was lousy, it was uncomfortable, it was tragic, but it was over. He couldn't bring back the dead any more than he could fly like Superman. At least he didn't feel responsible for the wasted deaths.

He had avenged the dead cops at the Star Market. The bartender had shot Tim Marchelli. Collins had finally killed Browne. None of it was his fault, it was just that he had never been in control. Somebody had been pulling his strings and punching his buttons all along. That frustrated him. That made him angry.

Harry stalked into the Holiday Inn without asking for messages. He went upstairs and packed, his mind preoccupied with things Californian. He was about to close his bag when he noticed something was missing.

It was a pair of slacks, some pants he had bought a few months ago in San Antonio while on a work trip. Harry looked in the closet and in the drawers until he realized what must have happened. Linda had had his cases overnight while he was getting beaten and had to go to the hospital. Being the domestic woman she was, she must have hung them up neatly in Shanna's old room until Peter had convinced her that Harry had to go.

Well, Harry reasoned, might as well kill two birds with one stone as Collins might say. He could say good-bye in

141

person while getting the slacks. Harry locked up his luggage, checked out, and got a taxi.

The Donovans lived in the bigotry capital of the Northeast, namely, South Boston. Harry mused about how Collins had described it. He must have known full well that Harry's cousins lived there while he was condemning the place.

Looking out the taxi window, Callahan had to admit the visual prospects weren't promising. The first thing he saw after the "South Boston" sign was factories. Grim, gray factories belching smoke into the blue ocean sky. Beyond that was a city that reminded him of Baltimore or Pittsburgh. Rundown, lower-middle-class houses riffling right against each other like a worn pack of cards.

On every block in downtown Boston, there was at least one little bistro and a decent place to eat. In Southie all there was were Donut Shops and fast-food joints for as far as the eye could see. Then the cab was beyond that section and entering the waterfront part of town.

It looked like the real estate developers had tried but failed. It looked like they had built the best condominiums they could on the loot they had and had hoped for the best. The best never came. The developers ran out, the money ran dry, and the buildings were running down.

The Donovans' place was on the beach. It was a square apartment building that looked like a couple of giant, prefabricated shoeboxes placed one on top of the other. There were no swimmers or sunbathers on the beach. There were just empty beer bottles and cans to mark where they had been. It was the most dismal beach front Callahan had ever seen. He began to think he should've called to say so long and kissed the slacks good-bye.

The taxi stopped in front of the cracked walk. Harry paid, got out, and walked between all the retirees rocking in the beach chairs on the lawn to the apartment house foyer. An old lady was coming out so Harry didn't have to go through the buzzer routine to get in. He held the

142

door open so the old woman with the walker could move slowly past him.

"Thank you, young man," she said.

The day wasn't a total loss, Harry figured. It had been quite some time since anyone had considered him a "young man." He rode up in an elevator, which was about as slow as the lady with the walker. It lurched from floor to floor, most of the bulbs behind the floor-marking numbers not lighting. It bounced to a tentative stop on the eighth floor. As the doors opened with a jolt, Harry saw faded numbers and arrows on the wall opposite him. According to them, the Donovans' apartment was all the way down the hall to the left.

The walls were thin, and the doors were of cheap wood. It would've been a cat burglar's paradise if there had been anything to steal. As it was, Harry could hear conversations in each dwelling as he passed them.

He stopped at the end of the hall in front of the Donovans' door. He was about to knock when he heard the unmistakable sounds of a barely controlled argument.

"We should have told him," Linda whined. "She's our daughter."

"She's not my daughter!" Peter roared, the sound of falling cutlery following his shout. "That miserable prick-sucking cunt. She's no daughter of mine!"

Linda broke down into tears. "No matter what she's done," she wailed. "She's still our daughter."

"I say no!" There were more crashes from within. Callahan's feeling of *déjà vu* returned. This was how the case had started, only then he had been listening to Morrisson, Sherman, and the Donovans' daughter, the one Peter seemed so vicious about disowning. Harry lowered his fist. He would listen a bit more.

"She's your daughter," the man seethed at his sobbing wife. "You're all alike, sucking up to other men, wiggling your goddamn asses at other men. Shoving your goddamn tits in other men's faces!"

143

Linda's voice was like a crushed little girl's. "How can you say that?" she barely managed to get out. "When it was you. . . . When it was you. . . ."

"I don't want to hear it!" Peter absolutely screamed.

"You'll have to hear it," Linda came back, her voice growing strength once she realized she had hit a pain center. "You'll have to admit the truth! Shanna . . . our daughter went to that man because you . . . !"

Harry heard the table go crashing over and Linda's scream just before he identified the sound of flesh hitting flesh. He heard Peter shrieking "I'll kill you! I'll kill you, you goddamn cunt!"

Then Harry kicked down the door.

Chapter Nine

The partition disappeared around Harry's flying foot. It was hardly strong enough to stand up against a hard rain, let alone a kick from the seasoned inspector. Instead of breaking the lock and the door swinging in, Harry's leg went right through the cheap material. It was an awkward and painful position. Harry threw his torso forward to smash through the rest of the way. The door frame stayed shut, just a hole the size of Callahan's body opened up.

Peter Donovan hardly noticed the interruption. He had one meaty hand around Linda's neck, and he was slapping her back and forth with the other. She was trying to tear at his hair while beating at the arm around her throat.

"That's enough!" Harry shouted, moving into the combination kitchen, living, and dining room.

Harry's voice brought Peter back to reality. But it was not the reality of a quiet, gentle husband taking care of his wife and daughter. It was the reality of a frustrated, failed, violent man who wanted to lash out at anything that got in his way. He stopped hitting Linda and looked up at Callahan with an evil, expectant grin.

"Well, well, well," he said. "Look who we have here. If it isn't the women's knight in shining armor." Callously, casually, Peter threw his wife aside. She slammed against the wall and sunk to the floor, crying and rubbing her bruised neck. "You're just what the doctors ordered,

'Dirty' Harry. Come on, let's see who can really fight dirty around here."

Donovan hunched over like a charging bull and made circular "come on" motions with both hands.

"Forget it," Harry said, standing up straight in the two-foot hallway behind the broken door. But while he said it, he checked out the room. The kitchenette was on the other side of the wall from him. The kitchen table was lying on its side next to Linda. The rug started there and stretched twenty feet across the way to a sliding door out onto the patio. Between the two points were a card table, a TV, a sofa, and a rectangular dining table.

"What are you going to do to stop me?" Peter barked. "Shoot me with your big .44 Magnum?" He laughed. "Come on, little man, let's see what you can do without your cannon." Peter charged with all the delighted abandon of an experienced streetfighter.

Harry moved into the room at the same time. They met right next to the stove.

Callahan's initial instinct was to drive the flat of his hand between Peter's clutching fingers and crush the man's nose back into his face, but at the last minute he restrained himself. No matter how big a bastard Donovan was, Harry didn't think Linda wanted to be a widow. There was a possibility of driving the nose bone right into the brain.

Instead, Peter slammed his head into Harry's torso, and Harry slammed both fists against the big Mick's ears.

Roaring with pain, Peter tried to bring his head up under Callahan's chin. Harry put both hands on the top of Donovan's head, jammed his leg between both of Peter's, and pushed. Donovan's upward momentum was channeled into a backward force. His arms flailed out, and he fell back, smashing off two of the upset kitchen table's legs.

Harry moved farther into the long room as Peter

grabbed one of the broken wooden stumps and charged with it over his head. Callahan's mind went back to the Police Academy's first year of self-defense training. Peter brought the makeshift club down. Harry caught his wrist in his left hand, grabbed the same arm's elbow with his right, pivoted, turned, and pulled.

The shoulder flip still worked like a charm after all these years. Donovan somersaulted over Harry's head and landed back-first on the card table. The whole room shook with his fall. The air was knocked out of him as the second table's spindly legs all broke at once. The heavy chair leg skittered out of Peter's hand and under the couch as he bounced on the hard floor and rolled, groaning, onto his side.

Normally, Harry would have kicked him in the back of the head to make sure he stayed down. Unfortunately, this wasn't a pimp, pusher, rapist, robber, or killer. It was just an incredible asshole who happened to be a relation. Harry was glad all his close family were dead. They wouldn't want to see what Linda had come to.

Harry turned his back on the dazed, cringing man and went to see how Linda was. She was in even a worse way than she had been in the orange Pinto. Not only couldn't she talk between tears, she wouldn't even look at Harry. She just kept waving him away with her head turned toward the wall.

Callahan felt Peter's second attack before he saw it. The floor under his feet vibrated. He smelled alcohol. He swung round to see Peter attempting a roundhouse right. Harry ducked under it. It sunk right into the plaster of the wall. Harry jerked his elbow forward into Donovan's chin. The man's head snapped back, and he stumbled against the sink.

Harry made the mistake of giving the man room again. Peter immediately dug his hand into a kitchen drawer and came out with a carving knife. Callahan turned around and ran to the couch. Playtime was over. Donovan was

147

getting seriously stupid. When he saw Harry run back, a smug smile grew across the bottom of his face. The look winked out when Harry stood his ground and pointed the Magnum barrel right between Peter's eyes.

"Now I know what you're thinking," Harry said, the words feeling comfortable and familiar. "You're thinking, 'He won't shoot me. I'm family.' Well, being that this *is* a .44 Magnum and could blow you hand clean off, you've got to ask yourself one question. Do I feel lucky?" Harry paused a beat. "Well? Do you, asshole?"

Harry was afraid the Mick would be too stubborn to back down. He was right. The look in Peter's eye said he didn't care what Harry said, the cop wouldn't shoot him. Donovan brought the knife in low and charged for the third time. Harry immediately pulled the trigger.

The Magnum's concussion in the cheap condo room was equal to that of a thunderclap. The flash and shell shaving stung Peter's face. It was such a monumental sound right in front of him that he was sure he was hit. He practically felt the shock wave of the lead smashing into him.

Only the bullet went over his right shoulder and into the refrigerator. It was Donovan's expectations that stopped his charge and threw him back in shock. Linda's frightened scream could only be heard after the .44's reverberation faded, and then it was too late to do anything about it.

Harry tossed the gun behind him onto the couch. He moved forward and slapped the knife out of Peter's hand. Then he punched the man across the jaw as hard as he could.

Donovan's feet left the floor as he twisted around in midair from the force of the blow. He landed unsteadily on his feet just as Harry buried his other fist into Peter's stomach. The man doubled over with a painful whoosh. Harry grabbed him by the ear and the nose. With a skin-tearing tug he hurled the big man over the sofa.

Peter smashed hard into the rug. He rolled over to the picture window.

Harry calmly walked around the couch, grabbed Peter by the shirt front, and brought him to his feet.

"Never pull a knife on me," Callahan said, both as a warning and as an explanation. Then he slammed a final fist right in the center of Donovan's face. The Mick shot back and through the patio picture window.

The glass blew out like cannon shot. It, too, was the cheapest grade. Peter crashed down with it, half-in and half-out of the room. Harry turned his back on the unconscious man, retrieved his gun, and went back to Linda.

The woman was on her feet, pointing in astonishment at the motionless body of her husband and screeching in short gasps. Harry swept her pointing finger out of the way and slapped her hard across the face. She suddenly stopped yelling and looked at Harry, blinking.

He grabbed her upper arms and shook her. "Six people are dead, Linda," he said in her face. "What should you have told me?"

She just stared at his face uncomprehendingly for a few more seconds. Then she started to cry again.

Harry shook her again, harder this time. "Don't cry," he demanded. "Tell me now. What you should have said."

They both heard a noise from the door. Harry turned to see three or four neighbors standing in the wreckage of the door.

"Uh, Linda," said an old woman in the lead. "Is there any trouble here? Anything we can do?"

"No, thank you, Mrs. O'Neill," Harry heard Linda say. He turned to see that the woman had collected herself. The interest of the neighbors did the trick. She could act the simpering fool in front of loved ones, but she had to put up a good front for the neighbors. "My husband and my cousin just had a little disagreement, that's all."

The old woman nodded with understanding, even amid the broken furniture, glass, and spreadeagled Peter. She turned to shoo the others back into the hall. Before she left herself, she turned to Harry.

"Good for you," she told him.

The old lady's calm had given Linda strength. But it wouldn't hold up if they stayed in the apartment. She got her coat out of the closet and walked toward the door.

"Come on, Harry," she said. "We have to get to town."

Within minutes, they were back in the Pinto, heading toward Boston. Tears were pouring down Linda's cheeks, but she was in control. They were the empty, bitter tears spilled over a wasted life. They were the remorseful drops of self-pity and self-loathing. She was crying over what could have been but never would be. She wasn't going to waste her breath over it.

"I wrote you without Peter knowing," she began, her knuckles white on the steering wheel. "It was before the Halliwell girl was killed, but our lives were already falling apart. I . . . I needed somebody to talk to. Someone who could protect me from Peter's violent rages."

"So he's beaten you before."

Linda felt she didn't have to answer that. Instead, she tried to explain the love she felt for him. "He doesn't hate me, Harry. He's burning up with self-hate. He just can't express it in any other way but rage."

"Don't defend him to me," Harry said flatly. "Go on."

"He had an affair," Linda intoned as if that sentence was the most important four words in the English language. "He was eating himself up with guilt about it. When Shanna found out, she went a little crazy. She started experimenting with all sorts of things and tried to find men she knew would punish her father. . . ."

Harry was beginning to lose her. Why would Shanna react so badly to her father's affair? There was no great bond between the two beforehand, and the girl was old enough to understand and handle her father's indiscretions. . . .

Then it hit him. The whole twisted chain of events locked into Harry's mind. "Pull over!" he shouted.

"What?" Linda blurted, surprised.

"Stop the car. Pull over." Harry checked the traffic situation around them, then grabbed the wheel himself and jerked it to the right. Linda hadn't even braked the vehicle all the way when Harry was out of the passenger's side and running toward the driver's seat through the kicked-up dust. "Move over," Harry commanded, pulling open the door and dropping down behind the steering wheel. He revved the engine and lurched back onto the road.

Callahan drove, thought, and talked furiously. "Shanna used to drop over a lot more often. She'd sometimes bring her friends along with her, wouldn't she? And being so beautiful, it wasn't unusual that her friends would be beautiful."

Linda didn't say anything. She just watched and held onto the armrest as the truth poured out of Harry's mouth. "He had an affair with *Christine*. So Shanna found a man she knew would drive Peter crazy. A man who would drive any bigoted Southie crazy. But it couldn't be just anyone. Even for revenge, Shanna's standards were too high to pick just anyone. It had to be an educated, entertaining, handsome man. An educated, entertaining, handsome *black* man."

Harry roared across the South Boston bridge into the heavily congested North End. The tires steamed and squealed as he sped onto Route 80 and into the tunnel under South Station.

"How long has Collins been coaching you?" he asked as the tunnel's yellow lights whipped by, creating a strobe effect inside the car.

"Since Judy Halliwell died," Linda admitted. "Peter

and he had called a truce to fight a common enemy, the Orenda cult. Shanna had dropped Christopher by then for Jeff Browne."

"What did Collins say? How did he describe the situation?"

"He said Shanna's life was in danger. He said that the Indian cult was a blood cult. That they were working up to a human sacrifice. He said that Judy's death proved that."

"Oh my God," Harry literally groaned. A plot had pieced together in his mind. A nearly unbelievable plot. But the frightening thing was that it held together. It held together better than the whole virgin-sacrifice concept.

"We're going to Shanna's apartment," he told his cousin. "No matter what happens, get her out of there. Take the car and bring her someplace safe. Drag her out by force if you have to, but get her the hell out of the line of fire!"

Harry wrenched the car over to the Copley Square exit, the Pinto's tires squealing in anguish. He turned sharply down Tremont Street, soared past the Public Gardens to Charles, swerved left, then sped to Mount Vernon Street. A left there, then another right, and they were in front of Shanna's corner building. Harry was out before the car had completely skidded to a stop. And before anyone inside could react to the rubber screeching, he had the Magnum in his hand and his foot up.

Without faltering, Harry kicked open the cellar apartment door. Two figures sat up in bed. He pointed the .44 at the first one—Christopher Collins.

"Is this the celebration you wanted to take me to?" Harry asked coldly.

The black detective was speechless until Linda came running in. "You talked!" Collins cried accusingly.

"Mother," Shanna spat, sitting up half-naked in the bed. "You told him!"

"Get your clothes on," Harry interrupted. Shanna just stared at him as if he were a dancing bear. He reached over and grabbed her wrist. "I said get your clothes on!" Harry pulled her right up and over the black man. She grabbed the sheet as she went, pulling it right off the bed. Harry threw the redhead at her mother, Shanna trying to wrap the sheet around her nudity.

Collins was only wearing his boxer shorts.

"Yeah," spat Harry. "She told me all right. You made this case, Collins. You had yourself assigned to the Halliwell murder just so you could get back with your lady love. Judy Halliwell wasn't even a member of the Order of the Orenda, for God's sake! But you played on everyone's fear of cults to blow it into a full-scale sect conspiracy."

"Now, wait a minute, Harry," the detective said nervously. "You've got no proof of that."

"No," Harry agreed distastefully. "What I have proof of is how you used the Donovans to control me. You told them that you had to handle everything if Shanna was going to get out alive. You told them not to give me any details if they wanted things to come out right. You wanted her, didn't you? You wanted this special white woman bad, didn't you? She'd give you respectability, wouldn't she? And the hierarchy would have to accept you then because she was one of them. A Southie."

"Callahan, you're raving. You're going crazy, Callahan," Collins babbled.

"So what did you do to get her, Collins? You sure kept everyone informed about the progress of the case, huh?"

"Chris didn't tell me anything!" Shanna spoke up, still clutching the sheet around her form.

Harry glanced at her, careful to keep the Magnum steadily aiming at Collins' chest. "You didn't hear me right the last time we talked, Shanna," he reminded her. "I said a Brookline waitress had died. You called her a blonde waitress. There were only two ways you could have known that. First, the murderer told you. At the time, I thought that was Jeff Browne. I thought Browne was coming to visit you that time.

"But then I got to thinking. Browne had a .44 slug in his shoulder. How the hell could he fool around with you? You were undressed to kill, Shanna. Nobody makes themselves up to be that attractive just to skip around the house. So there was one other person in one piece who could've told you that."

Harry stared pointedly at Collins.

"All right!" the detective shouted. "OK, so I told everybody a few things. So things worked out for the best, didn't they? We got the killer, didn't we?"

Callahan stepped toward him. Collins jumped back to huddle against the wall.

"You followed me after that first night," he seethed.

"No!"

"You told Christine where to find me."

"No. Harry, I swear. . . ."

"What else did you do, Collins? How far would you go to get ahead? Kidnap and drug a girl after killing her boyfriend?"

Collins' dark eyes widened. He could see the noose Harry was tightening around his neck.

"Would you kill another innocent girl just to frame the suspect?"

"Jesus Christ, Harry. Stop it. Stop it now."

"Would you pump your captive so full of drugs she didn't know who was holding her hostage? Would you get your hands on Browne and do the same to him?"

"Harry, you don't know what you're saying!" Collins cried, crawling up the wall. "No, man, you got it all wrong!"

Harry yelled over his denials. "Would you set up a whole sacrificial scene just so I could kill the suspect? And when I didn't, you were there to play the cavalry?"

"This has gone far enough . . . !" Shanna declared, suddenly walking between Collins and the gun.

But Collins knew Callahan's reputation better than the girl did. He knew Harry had the clout to make any arrest

154

stick. And he knew that Harry was right in that this new chain of events had more logic than the cult story. Police corruption was so commonplace that the courts would buy almost anything. Just as the girl drew near, Collins grabbed her by the hair and around the waist. He used her as a shield as he ran out the door.

Harry gave chase, but Shanna just stood in the doorway after Collins had released her. Harry nearly punched her out of the way. Shanna saw his muscles tense and flinched. Harry stopped himself for the second time that day and just pulled Shanna back into the apartment by the shoulder.

"Get her out of here," he told Linda. "And call the police!"

Harry tore after the black man in the white boxer trunks. Things had changed from the sixties. If a negro had run around any major city in his underwear ten years ago, he would have been tackled by twenty concerned citizens before he had gotten ten yards. Everyone would have assumed that he was running from the police. In the eighties, a man in trunks running as fast as he could was not unusual. Everyone would think that he was just another jogger. For one of the few times, Harry wished it was the sixties again.

Collins turned onto Beacon Street and ran up to the first corner. The light was only with him one way, so he took a left. Attached to the building across the street was a fire escape. Collins leaped up onto the first rung and started climbing.

Harry might have been able to hit him from the angle and the distance. But again something was keeping him from pulling the trigger. He had never shot a man unless it was in self-defense or he was absolutely sure about the guilt. As he crossed Beacon Street toward the fire escape, he had to admit he wasn't sure. His theory made more sense than the Orenda plot, but then anything would.

Harry jumped onto the third fire escape rung, still clenching the .44 in his right hand but not aiming it. By then, Collins had reached the roof. He kept running without looking back. Harry pumped his legs harder. He had to get to the end of it. He couldn't let Collins get away. He had to find out the truth.

Callahan dragged himself to the roof as fast as he could. He pulled himself over the roof lip just as Collins was leaping from one building to the next. The athletic black soared across a ten-foot span onto the tar of the brownstone next door. This time Harry did aim the weapon.

"Halt," he said. Collins ducked behind a chimney. Harry purposefully pulled the trigger. The Magnum bucked in his hand, and the bullet slashed across the bricks of the fireplace tube. Collins started zigzagging across the other roof. Harry ran to the edge of the first building and jumped. He landed on the upraised lip of the second roof's edge and fell forward. He rolled and came up running again.

Collins leaped to the next roof. They were playing leap frog across the tops of the Beacon Street townhouses. Harry stopped in the middle of the second roof and aimed at Collins' churning legs. He could see that the black's bare feet were already torn and bleeding.

With an eight and three-eighths-inch Magnum barrel, there'd be a good chance he'd be able to wing the detective. But with the slightly less velocity ability of the six and a half, it was chancy. Harry decided to chance it anyway. He pulled the trigger, the gun jumped, and the bullet tore a hunk out of the black man's thigh.

With a pained shout, Collins skipped, stumbled, and fell right on the opposite edge of the third building. At that moment, Harry heard the sounds of police sirens screaming up the street. There was one thing nice about a battle between a Boston detective and a San Francisco inspector; it brought the rest of the force out damn quick.

Harry slowed as he neared the edge of his roof. He kept the .44 centered on Collins back as the man crawled to the front edge of the third building.

"Hey," he screamed down at the squad cars, waving madly. "Hey, up here! Up here!"

The same feeling Harry had when he nearly shot the couple in the car instead of Browne returned to him with almost full intensity. Collins was calling the cops. He wanted their help. He hadn't run because he thought Harry was going to turn him in. He ran because he thought Harry was going to kill him!

Callahan didn't have a chance to think any more about it after that. Because the Boston policemen got out of their cars and started shooting at him.

Chapter Ten

The whole area around Harry's feet seemed to erupt. His arms went up to protect his face as the tar of the roof, bricks on surrounding chimneys, and the metal on all the TV antennae started whinning, splitting, breaking, and flying off in all directions. The chips and shards dug into Harry's skin as he spun down to his face.

Well, of course, these guys would be shooting at him, Harry told himself angrily. All they got in their patrol cars was an "officer needs assistance" code. And as far as the majority of the Boston PD was concerned, Collins was the officer—in or out of uniform. After all, it was Collins' face that was plastered on every TV and newspaper in the city after the press conference, not Callahan's.

Harry looked wildly around for a way out as the police bullets continued to slam into the surface around him. He figured he had nothing to fear immediately. The cops wouldn't risk the lives of the tenants by shooting too low. But in a matter of minutes, if they were any good at all, a cop would appear on the fire escape of the first building, a cop would appear from the fire escape in the last building, a cop would crawl up the fire escape on this building, and a few more would be working their way up the stairs right below Harry. He couldn't trust Collins to call them off. It might fit the detective's plan to have

Harry killed. He had to work fast if he wasn't going to be perforated.

Callahan hastily crawled to the edge of the roof opposite the fire escape and looked down. There was a window on the third floor directly across from a third floor window in the next building. He looked around the roof for a door to a stairwell and saw it on the northwest edge of the building.

He risked rising to a crouch to run for it. He had just gotten his hand on the latch when an officer armed with an M-16 jumped onto the last building's roof from the fire escape.

Oh God, Harry thought. The cop thinks he's a SWAT member. Harry shot in his general direction just to keep him down. Then he hauled back the metal door and dove through. He slid face first down the first staircase as thirteen M-16 slugs made a circular design in the metal work of the roof door. As his face touched the third-floor carpet, Harry heard more cops pounding up to the second-floor landing.

Callahan got his bearings quickly. He found the door he was looking for, then leaned over the banister in front of it and started firing at the policemen below. He kept shooting until he heard them retreat to the first floor and the Magnum's hammer clicked on a spent shell.

The cops below heard it, too. They doubled their speed up the steps. Their noise covered the sound of Harry kicking the door in. He jumped into the apartment and swung the door shut behind him, hoping the place was empty. No such luck. A petrified college student stood in the doorway to his bathroom, his pants down.

Harry lowered his gun, reached into his pocket, and took out a wad of bills. "You can have all this money if you don't shout," he told the embarrassed kid. Without waiting for an answer, he ran into the apartment's bedroom, threw back the shades, and opened the window on the side wall. It wasn't big enough. He closed it again and moved back to the bedroom door.

The kid was still staring in wide-eyed wonder at the cop. As Harry seemed to decide against whatever he was planning to do, the kid opened his mouth to ask a question. But then Harry ran as fast as he could in the other direction. He took three long strides and propelled himself through the window as hard as he could.

As the glass smashed around his head and folded arms, Harry sure hoped his trajectory was right. If he caught any part of the opposite wall, there'd be a long fall to Beacon Street.

He felt something smash into his side. After a split second, it gave way. Harry had done it. He had jumped across the alley through two closed windows.

He felt something sliding across his knees as he landed. He couldn't push his legs straight. He looked down to see himself sliding across a table, taking most of some very surprised people's lunches with him. He finally fell off the edge of the long surface, rolled, and came up at the door of the apartment.

"Sorry," he said hastily to the four people half-out of their seats. Then he slammed the door behind him and went in search of a back way.

Timing was still important. With luck, the kid had kept his peace. If the cops didn't know he'd changed buildings the hard way, they wouldn't have enough men to cover all the block's exits yet. But it was only a matter of minutes before they cordoned off the entire area.

Callahan found the back stairway. He went down until he found the basement door. It let out onto an alleyway between blocks. He saw no cops either way, so he crossed to a basement door on the opposite side and kicked it open. He walked through the building's lobby and came out on Newbury Street.

He kept walking quickly without looking back. He still wasn't in the clear, not by a long shot. He didn't want the police to find him, and he didn't want to give up so they could compare theories. He needed time to think. Someplace other than a police station.

He couldn't return to Linda's or Shanna's apartment. That would be the first and second place they would look. He couldn't go to Christine's place. That would be the third place they'd look. Harry turned right up Newbury Street. There was only one other place he knew about for sure in Boston. And that was Shanna's college counselor's office—Dr. Gerrold.

Callahan moved quickly to the door in between the record store and cheese shop. He checked his watch. It was perfect timing. Just after five and closing time. He hoped the doctor would be out. Callahan trotted up the steps. On the first landing was a door to a chiropractor's office. On the second was the sign for a professional medium. On the third and last was a legend which read: "Dr. Richard Gerrold. Students: M-W-F 3 to 8 P.M. All others by appointment."

Behind the opaque glass the office was dark. Harry brought out his trusty credit card again. It didn't work. Someone had installed a metal trim bar to prevent just such an occurrence. Callahan was undaunted. From the same wallet he had taken the card, he pulled out a thin metal rod. A few minutes at the top of the stairs and the lock clicked open and the door swung back.

The office was decked out very nicely. It had a comfortable, welcome, and private feeling. Three things Harry appreciated at this stage of the game. He relocked the door, leaned his back against it, and rubbed his face. Dropping his hands and sighing, Callahan tried to make his mind work again. It told him he was hungry. He began to prowl around the office for something to eat. He found a small refrigerator with a carton of orange juice and a red raspberry yogurt cup. He took both and moved toward the oak door opposite the receptionist's desk marked "Private."

He put down the yogurt and drank the O.J. while trying the knob. It was locked. The credit card worked on this one. Inside was an even classier room than the reception area. There was a big, walnut desk in the middle and a luxuriously appointed couch off to the side. All around those were bookcases filled with psychology volumes, spotlights, file cabinets, the latest in recording equipment, and a small locked cabinet that looked like it served as a bar.

Harry sat behind the desk, shook the yogurt canister vigorously, took the lid off, and drank it. He didn't feel much better afterward, but at least it took an edge off his hunger. It let him think.

If Callahan was right about Collins, then the police would have one of the more insidious mass murderers in the city's history under arrest. If he was wrong, then Harry was guilty of what he had accused Morrisson of: assault with a deadly weapon, resisting arrest, and disturbing the peace. Not to mention several other charges.

And just as before, Harry wasn't positive he was right. The danger might be over, but the crime had not been completely solved. God, he groaned to himself, what a mess. Stuck in an Eastern city two thousand miles away from any possible character witnesses, with the police force after him. He had nearly killed his cousin's husband. He had shot two of his beloved relative's lovers and seen four other people die. And still he was no closer to any kind of peace of mind.

He needed a drink. Badly. He swung up to the cabinet, pulling out his metal pick as he rose. The lock was small and simple. Harry broke it in a matter of seconds. The small wooden side folded down into a little shelf. Inside was a junkie's paradise.

There were vials of liquid in neat little rows. There were three separate syringes in their own individual velour cases. There was a brass cup full of needles, each individually wrapped and sanitized.

The hair actually stood up on the back of Harry's neck. A long row of test tubes filled with fluid were marked with the initials "C.S." A shorter row was labeled

"S.D." The shortest of all had "J.B." There were other initials Harry didn't recognize. It hardly made a difference. Harry turned toward the files with his mouth open.

He walked over like a zombie. He vaguely recalled what Shanna had said when he had walked her here the first time. "Everybody at Emerson has one." Everybody? Including Christine Sherman, Jeff Browne, Tom Morrisson, and Judy Halliwell?

Harry tore through the entire office like a man possessed. He found all the records. Everyone involved with the Orenda investigation had been scheduled for counseling sessions with Gerrold. Harry took some of the vials, wrapped them in Kleenex from a handy box, and put them in his pocket. He'd be very interested to see the chemical breakdown in the police lab.

In fact, Harry found everything to make a case except one thing. Morrisson's hunting knife. The knife Harry was now sure had killed Halliwell, Monahan, Morrisson, and Bryant.

Callahan's head snapped up as he heard the key go into the furthermost door. The bolt opened, and the door swung in again, framing a slight, mustached, blond-haired man in the doorway. As soon as he saw the ransacked office, he turned to run. Harry shot him in the back. He was sure this time.

Richard Gerrold dove headfirst into the hallway wall. He managed not to fall down the steps by holding onto the banister. He slid face down the wall, leaving blood streaks and saliva marks in his wake. He turned so he could sit on his haunches. He blinked, opened and closed his mouth, and tried to adjust to the pain. Unbelievably he did not lose consciousness.

When Harry walked up, Gerrold looked at him and started laughing. Harry shrugged the files up farther under his arm and tightened his grip on the Magnum butt. He saw that the doctor's shoulder was almost completely shattered, yet the man remained conscious and laughing.

Callahan sat on the top step next to Gerrold. "What's so funny?" he asked lifelessly.

"Nothing," the slight, blond man chuckled, then winced from the pain. "It's just that I knew I'd never get away with it. I'm surprised it went on this long."

"So am I," Harry quietly admitted. "But you seem to have covered yourself very well."

"Ah, the human brain, Inspector," the blond man intoned. "It's such a delicate thing. Any, almost any, time the student's treatment could break down, and they would remember everything."

"Such as?" Harry prompted, looking down the long stairway.

"Oh, the rapes," Gerrold said lightly. "I took every single one of them on the couch in there. They don't even remember it. That's how I started. Rapes."

Gerrold had been a counselor at a campus in the Midwest. There, utilizing hypnosis and booster drugs, he had perfected a method of indulging his sexual appetite without risking rejection.

He was satisfied with that . . . at first.

"It got boring," Gerrold said wistfully. "I became fascinated with how far I could go. Just how much power I could hold over these girls. There's no such thing as hypnotism, you know. It's just a word we use to describe the combination of suggestion and the subject's imagination. The Amazing Kreskin has been saying that for years on television. And I've proven him right. Television has shaped an entire generation's imagination. Nothing is outside the realm of possibility now.

"You know the saying 'a hypnotized person will never do anything against their will?' It's true, but *nothing is against their will any longer*. Teenagers today have been inundated with so many news shows that package reality as fantasy, *they really don't care about the difference*. They'll watch the six o'clock news or *Magnum, P. I.,* they don't care.

"So if I tell them to go out and kill, they'll do it. They *did* it. They can't distinguish between real life and fiction."

The best subjects, Harry learned, were the already creative kids; the actors especially. They were used to taking on another character's traits and motivations. So when it came time to murder, their subconsciouses were telling them it was all part of a movie. Just like *Just Before Dawn.*

Harry let the man ramble on. It hardly made a difference now. The damage had already been done. He was only sorry they hadn't gotten to him sooner. If only Collins hadn't been so hot for a promotion and Shanna's body, the police might have put the connection together long before.

Gerrold was a power-mad, egocentric, perverted madman who was dangerous because he was so capable. He was the ultimate cult leader—a person who had discovered precise control over the most attractive subjects possible.

"It's a matter of selection," Gerrold mused, trying to stem the flow of blood from his mangled shoulder. "Both in the subject and in the timing. You can't control any one person all the time. You have to eliminate the hard cases and pick just the right moment to follow through on the initial treatments. This college position helped enormously."

"How did you get it?" Harry wanted to know.

"I had the credentials," Gerrold said pompously. "That's what I mean about timing. The majority of my career has been spent diagnosing real problems. Only when that special subject appears do I take advantage of the situation."

Callahan stood up. "All right, that's enough. Let's go."

Gerrold looked up innocently. "Where to?"

"You can tell the rest of the story at Police Headquarters."

Gerrold laughed anew. "But my dear man," he chortled. "You attacked me. You ransacked my office, then shot me in cold blood."

166

Harry ignored the line as wishful thinking. "Come on, no more games."

"You don't seem to understand, Inspector," the blond man explained patiently. "I've told you all this because I had to tell someone. But those chemicals and those files aren't enough in themselves to make an airtight case. You need corroborating witnesses. You need the victims to give evidence. And there are none. They're all dead."

Callahan's face and manner became very still. "What are you talking about?"

"Don't you understand? *I* didn't do anything. All the girls that I raped don't remember it, and there's no way they'll be able to say for sure that it happened. And they were far from being virgins. . . ."

"What about Halliwell?" Callahan asked quickly, wanting to know but dreading to hear.

"I'm telling you, Inspector. I didn't do anything."

"Then who did?" Harry exploded. "Morrisson? Browne? Monahan?"

"None of them." Gerrold confessed. "Monahan just happened to be in the wrong place at the wrong time. He witnessed Halliwell's murder, but he was not an active part of it. Browne was hard to control. If he hadn't been weakened by your shooting him, I would not have been able to arrange that little Indian ceremonial scene on Beacon Hill."

No wonder the man had been shaking and sweating, Harry recalled. He had been fighting something—fighting a predirected order. He had wanted to defend himself, but he couldn't shoot. Gerrold needed him dead. "And Morrisson?"

"Tom was impossible to control. He had to be killed immediately. He was the only one who seemed able to get through to Christine."

Callahan could have shot him then. But he needed to know more. "Christine," he breathed, dumbfounded.

"Yes," said Gerrold, "beautiful Christine. The prize of the bunch. She loved men. Any man. She felt other women were competition. She was willing, with the proper encouragement, to do anything. To anyone."

"Where is she?" Harry shouted in Gerrold's face.

"Not at home," the doctor said roguishly.

Harry ground his fist against the doctor's mashed shoulder. "Where is she?" he repeated.

Gerrold gasped in pain, and tears rolled out of his tightly closed eyes. "That's all right," he managed to grunt between clenched teeth. "I don't mind."

"Where is Christine?" Harry demanded, grinding the bone even harder.

"Use . . . your . . . head!" the slight man screamed. Callahan eased up immediately. "Where would she be? I told you that there will be no one left to testify against me. Think about it."

Harry did. He grabbed Gerrold under his arms and dragged him down the stairs. When they got to the bottom, Harry slammed him against the door and went through his pockets. He found the car keys on the second try. He recognized the shape of the key and the emblem on the key chain immediately.

"A BMW," Harry cursed. "Naturally you would drive a fucking BMW." He carried Gerrold out the door to the only BMW at the curb. He pushed the doctor against the roof of the car while he unlocked the door. "What in hell did you come back to the office for?"

Gerrold giggled grimly again. "I left a yogurt I wanted for dessert in the office fridge."

Harry couldn't help laughing himself this time, but it was a desperate laugh pushed out of his chest cavity by disbelieving pain. He practically threw Gerrold onto the seat. He slid over the hood and got in on the driver's side.

He jammed the car into gear, twisted the engine into life and burned rubber. Where would Linda bring Shanna for safety, Harry asked himself furiously. The only place he could think of was back at the condominium. Maybe in Mrs. O'Neill's apartment. Harry began to retrace his earlier drive to Linda's but at even greater speeds.

The rest of the story came out along the way. Every time Gerrold weakened and blacked out, Harry woke him. The doctor just couldn't seem to stop talking about it once he had started. Halliwell had been a thrill kill. He had asked Christine who she most wanted to stick it to. Under the treatment, she had said Judy.

"It made her sick, she said," Gerrold elaborated. "Judy was a beautiful girl, but she didn't do anything about it. That drove Christine crazier than if she had been a tease. She couldn't stand Judy's oblivious, unconcerned sexuality."

So Gerrold had sent Christine after her. Monahan had just happened by and had to die as a witness. Then the first problems began to arise. Morrisson had begun to break through the defenses Gerrold had set up in Christine's mind.

"That first day," the doctor said. "When you appeared? Thomas was trying to take the knife away from her, not stab her with it. In his agitated state, when he saw you barreling toward him, he ran. He couldn't believe his girl was a killer so he kept silent until it was too late."

"You followed me," Harry realized. "You gave Christine my number!"

"It wasn't easy. We had to check every police station in town. But we finally lucked out, and there you were. Detective Collins was kind enough to drop you off in the neighborhood, so shadowing you from then on was child's play."

"And you were the one who knocked me out in the Emerson building."

"That was the one thing I did do."

But not before more trouble cropped up. Killing Morrisson had been a major trauma for the girl, treatment or no treatment. Gerrold couldn't get her to attack Harry, so he had to knock her out and do the dirty work himself.

"After that I kept her at my house until she was

needed," Gerrold elaborated. "It was wonderful!" he said with conviction. "You don't know real power, Inspector, until you have a beautiful woman mewling and struggling at your feet in complete helplessness."

Collins had done all the rest. When Gerrold saw the "blood cult" pattern emerging, it fit right in with his victims and plans. When he needed another "sacrifice" to frame Browne in his apartment, he delved into Christine's subconscious again. The Sherman girl had only visited that Brookline bar once, but she didn't like the waitress because her blonde hair had stood out more in the dark bar interior. That was the reason Cathy had died in such shock. She could not comprehend that another woman was raping her.

"With Shanna gone, it will all be over," Gerrold said sadly. "The circle will be complete. No victims left. All gone."

"What about Christine?" Callahan interjected, speeding into Southie.

"But that's what makes it perfect, don't you see? She won't remember. And even if someone is able to break through the intense blocks I created while she was captive, it is she who conceived and executed the murders. She picked the victims, and she killed them! Gerrold looked slyly up at Harry. "You know Peter Sellers' last great movie, *Being There?* It was about a man who essentially became someone else. His name was Chauncey Gardner, and he was right. It is more fun to watch."

Harry turned the corner onto the street where the Donovans lived. The entire road was crawling with police cars. By the time Harry rammed through the roadblock, it was too late to stop. Cops on all sides started pouring into the street, pulling out their weapons as they came. Harry swerved the responsive Bavarian-made sports car up onto the left sidewalk, near the beach wall.

If he could just turn onto the lawn and drive through the entrance, he might be able to get under cover before the police blasted him.

It was wishful thinking. He saw the gun flashes. He heard the bullets careen across the car body. He was just about to duck under the dashboard when two side tires blew.

The BMW was a great car and Harry was an experienced chase driver, but no one could have controlled it in that situation. Harry felt the vehicle slam against the sea wall sideways at high speed. He saw a wave of sparks sear off from the door next to him. He heard the grinding, rending tear of metal being ripped off the driver's side of the body.

He wrenched the wheel back and forth while slamming the brakes to the floor. The car began to slew sideways. Harry released the brake and spun the wheel. The one good front tire held on and the car turned all the way around. He slammed the accelerator down again. The rubber sent up gouts of smoke as the four-wheel drive tried to countereffect the backward momentum. Harry's action was the only thing that saved both men's lives when the car crashed into a bend in the stone sea wall.

The headrests saved them from whiplash or a broken neck. The car was going slow enough so they weren't killed on impact and fast enough to propel the car up and lazily over the stone wall onto the beach. It crashed down on its side and then sluggishly turned upright again.

Harry's head had slammed against the side window and the steering wheel. He could barely see the flames once the car caught fire. He tried to clear his head. He tried to move. He could do neither.

He was at least able to see. He found himself looking at Dr. Richard Gerrold, holding Harry's Magnum in his good hand. "Now that we've talked," Gerrold said affably, the engine flames flickering in back of his head, "I feel it might be a good idea if you were dead."

At point-blank range, with Harry unable to do anything about it, the slight, blond doctor pulled the Magnum's trigger with his left forefinger.

By that time his aim was already off. The .44 Magnum

is a cannon. A great deal of strength is needed to shoot and control it. Gerrold didn't have it.

By the time the hammer came down on the shell, the barrel was pointing two inches from Harry's head. When the lead was blasted out, the resulting report nearly broke Gerrold's wrist. The gun bucked up right into the doctor's face, slashing one of his eyes.

The bullet shattered the cracked glass behind Harry's head. It deafened and nearly blinded him. When he could hear again, he heard the crackle of the car flames getting stronger. He heard the wails of Gerrold as he tried to push his torn eye back into its socket.

Callahan groped forward like a blind man. He found the Magnum on the dashboard. With his other hand he felt for Gerrold's face. His finger sunk into the ruined eye. Gerrold contorted in excruciating pain, his mouth wide open. Harry stuck his hand in the mouth. He pulled the writhing doctor back to the seat. By touch only he shoved the Magnum barrel deep into Gerrold's mouth.

He pulled the trigger, only hearing the doctor's perverted brains splashing onto the back seat.

Harry turned his head toward the sound of the ocean. Light was coming through. He crawled out of the broken window and onto the sand. He pulled himself up and ran for the sound of the waves. When the BMW's gas tank exploded, he had run far enough away so he wasn't killed.

But he was thrown forward by the shock wave. When he rose to his elbows again and opened his eyes, he could see clearly. He looked behind him to see the burning structure of the fancy car and a bunch of cops bearing down on him, led by Christopher Collins.

"Where's Shanna?" he shouted angrily at Harry.

"Isn't she here?" he asked, getting up.

"No," Collins said, coming right up in front of the San Francisco inspector. "What the hell did you do with her?"

"Did you check all the apartments?" was Harry's answer.

"Everyone," Collins answered angrily. "Peter Donovan is in the hospital. He'll live, but he won't cooperate." The black man's anger left him. "Harry, what happened?" he said desperately. "Where is she?"

Callahan went through his mind as he had gone through the files of Gerrold's office. He went back to his very first conversation with Linda in almost ten years.

"Almost finished an apartment house in Revere," she had said.

Harry asked Collins. Collins knew. It was a retirement hotel that Donovan's company had only been able to complete the shell of. Because the incoming residents were going to be on fixed incomes, it was constructed of the cheapest materials. Even so, the money had run out. It had floors and ceilings on most floors, but many of the walls were missing.

The black detective got there in record time, Harry explaining on the way. By the time they arrived at the locked outside gate, Collins was sick with remorseful grief.

"She's dead," he said bitterly. "I've killed her." Harry ignored him. He leaned out the window of the car and blew the lock off the chain holding the gate closed. The gate swung out on its own accord. Collins drove right to the open-ended basement.

It was sunset. The red, purple, and yellow sky made up the structure's walls with light. They illuminated the small, torn body of Linda Donovan among the rubble of the basement. She lay with her eyes open, staring at the unfinished basement ceiling as the blood from her knife wounds painted the concrete floor.

She had tried. She thought she had come up with a clever place to be safe. But it was the one place Christine knew all too well. She had met Peter here constantly during their affair.

Harry saw two staircases, one on each side of the building. He pointed Collins toward the far one. He moved up the steps closest to Linda's body.

He found the two girls on the eighth floor. They were in a kitchen with the outside wall missing. Shanna was on her back on the floor. Christine was holding the hunting knife against Shanna's freckled neck as she drove inside the Donovan girl again and again.

It was a mockery of sex. The artificial sexual organ was strapped around the waist of the big coat Christine was wearing. She felt nothing through it, so she just kept jamming it between Shanna's legs with continuous thrusts of her hips. Shanna's neck was already marked with cuts from the unsteady knife.

Linda had saved her daughter after all. Christine had spent all her homicidal fury on the mother. She was merely expending her sexual frustrations on Shanna.

The redhead saw Harry first. She said his name in a pained hush. Christine stopped at the sound of the voice. She got up slowly and turned around. Harry was never so sickened. He futilely wished that Gerrold was still alive so he could torture him for as long as he had tortured the brunette.

Christine looked through Harry at first, then she recognized him and smiled. "So you've come," she said. She opened her arms and walked toward him.

Then she realized that she was not in her apartment. She looked around the room in bewilderment. Then she looked down at the blood-streaked dildo tied between her legs. She saw the stained knife in her hand. She looked back at Shanna, who was crying in a fetal position while a thin stream of blood ran across her thigh. That's all it took. Gerrold's mental blocks were weaker than the doctor had thought.

Christine's mouth opened. She moved back, away from both Harry and Shanna. Her face tried for an expression, but she couldn't find one. The disorientation had devastated all the Gerrold-built blocks. Suddenly, in her mind, the fantasy became reality again. The movie she had acted in for Director Gerrold was her real life. She had tortured. She had murdered. She had raped.

Her face was the most tragic Harry had ever seen. The beauty that had been there was ravaged, ruined, razed away.

"Kill me," she begged.

Harry raised the Magnum.

He had only killed people in self-defense or people who deserved it. The problem was did Christine deserve it? She had done it, but she was not to blame. The murder was inside her, but someone had brought out that murder that is inside everyone.

Harry hesitated still. Collins came rushing into the room, his gun out.

"No!" Harry shouted. "Get out! I don't want you here. I don't want you anywhere near Shanna again. I don't want to see you or hear about you. Get out and get the rest of the men."

The black detective saw that Shanna was still alive, so he did what he was told.

Harry and Christine faced each other for a few moments longer. Both were desperately looking for a way out. She came up with the solution first.

"Kill me," she said, "or I'll kill this girl." She said it softly, imploringly. She said it with peaceful conviction.

Harry pulled the trigger. Christine's body was thrown back and out the open wall. There was no scream as she fell. She had no lungs left to scream with. She landed ten feet from Linda's body.

Shanna got up and ran to Harry's arms. She shook silently in his embrace. Harry looked out at the sunset.

He never knew if Collins tried to see Shanna again. All he knew is that Collins never saw him again. He never knew whether Peter and Shanna got together again. He never knew what kind of funeral Linda had.

Dirty Harry Callahan left Boston the next morning and never went back.

MEN OF ACTION BOOKS

DIRTY HARRY By Dane Hartman

He's "Dirty Harry" Callahan—tough, unorthodox, no-nonsense plain-clothesman extraordinaire of the San Francisco Police Department... Inspector #71 assigned to the bruising, thankless homicide detail...A consummate crimebuster nothing can stop—not even the law! Explosive mysteries involving racketeers, murderers, extortioners, pushers, and skyjackers; savage, bizarre murders, accomplished with such cunning and expertise that the frustrated S.F.P.D. finds itself without a single clue; hair-raising action and violence as Dirty Harry arrives on the scene, armed with nothing but a Smith & Wesson .44 and a bag of dirty tricks; unbearable suspense and hairy chase sequences as Dirty Harry sleuths to unmask the villain and solve the mystery. Dirty Harry—when the chips are down, he's the most low-down cop on the case.

#1 DUEL FOR CANNONS	(C90-793, $1.95)
#2 DEATH ON THE DOCKS	(C90-792, $1.95)
#3 THE LONG DEATH	(C90-848, $1.95)
#4 THE MEXICO KILL	(C90-863, $1.95)

To order, use the coupon below. If you prefer to use your own stationery, please include complete title as well as book number and price. Allow 4 weeks for delivery.

WARNER BOOKS
P.O. Box 690
New York, N.Y. 10019

Please send me the books I have checked. I enclose a check or money order (not cash), plus 50¢ per order and 50¢ per copy to cover postage and handling.*

_____ Please send me your free mail order catalog. (If ordering only the catalog, include a large self-addressed, stamped envelope.)

Name _____

Address _____

City _____

State _____ Zip _____

*N.Y. State and California residents add applicable sales tax.